I0575642

NEVER NOT YOURS

K.V. THORN

THORN PUBLISHING HOUSE

NEVER NOT YOURS

January 2026

Published by Thorn Publishing House

ISBN 978-8-9938308-0-3 (PAPERBACK EDITION)

ISBN 978-8-99-38308-1-0 (EBOOK EDITION)

For the one I still dream about. For the memory I never meant to touch again but couldn't help tasting one last time.

This is for the hands that once held me, the lips that still burn on my skin, and the kind of love that was never safe, but always worth it.

"Touching him was like realizing all you ever wanted was right there in front of you" - Taylor Swift

AUTHOR'S NOTE

This story dives deep into complex emotions, relationships, and the kind of love that doesn't always follow the rules. Along the way, it explores themes of infidelity, emotional cheating, grief, marital conflict, separation, pregnancy-related distress, emotional manipulation, and mental health. It also includes sensual and sexually explicit scenes.

I wrote this book with honesty and heart, but I understand that some of these themes may be sensitive or triggering. Please take care of yourself while reading.

Your well-being is more important than finishing a chapter.

With all my heart, K. V. Thorn

THE PLAYLIST

Taylor Swift — Red

Gracie Abrams — Where Do We Go Now?

Taylor Swift — Daylight

Taylor Swift — imgonnagetyouback

Morgan Wallen — If You Were Mine

Taylor Swift — Guilty as Sin?

Taylor Swift — Dress

Hinder — Lips of an Angel

Taylor Swift — illicit affairs

Halsey — Colors

Taylor Swift — Right Where You Left Me

Taylor Swift — loml

Gracie Abrams — I'm Sorry, I Love You

Aerosmith, YUNGBLUD — My Only Angel

SPICY CHAPTER GUIDE

Chapter Five
Chapter Six
Chapter Eight
Chapter Nine
Chapter Thirteen
Chapter Fourteen
Chapter Fifteen
Chapter Sixteen
Chapter Eighteen
Chapter Twenty
Chapter Twenty Nine
Chapter Thirty
Chapter Thirty One
Chapter Thirty Two
Chapter Thirty Three

NEVER NOT YOURS

PROLOGUE
OLIVIA

Sixteen years ago

"I just don't think we can keep doing this, Liv."

My stomach dropped. Those were the words I was most afraid to hear him say. I knew this could happen. I knew that a year apart would change things. Long distance was supposed to be just a temporary thing, just a stupid test of time.

But this? Ending us? No. No.

I wanted to beg him. I wanted him to take back everything he said during this call. I wanted him to tell me to come over, to fix this the way we always did. But I didn't. I couldn't.

And neither did he.

"Fine, if that's what you want, okay." The tears burned down my cheeks. I'm so damn tired of crying, of feeling hopeless and small.

"It's not what I want, Liv, it's just...what we need to do." His voice cracked, but I couldn't tell if it was because he cared or because he didn't anymore. And I hated myself for it.

"No. This is what *you* need to do. I didn't ask for any of this. I was going to move there, for fuck's sake, Ethan. I told you this a year ago, and you agreed. So no, we don't '*need*' to do shit. But fine, I hope *you are* happy with your choice."

I ended the call with a pit in my stomach so deep it felt like it might swallow me. I wanted him. God, I wanted him more than anything in the world. But I couldn't beg. I wouldn't beg.

If he didn't love me anymore, then...fine. If he didn't want me, okay. That was on him. Not me.

I stared at my half-unpacked bags, clothes spilling out like they were mocking me. I had been so naive. Thinking we'd start our lives together. Thinking we'd finally move in, build something real outside of this town. Stupid, stupid, stupid.

We promised that I would apply to a college near him. Not the same one because we wanted to keep our experiences separated. My mom always told me not to compromise or change my life for a boy. So, in that sense, I listened to her. My plan was always to finish my senior year of high school, move there, and then get an apartment together in the second semester. We had everything planned out. He already had a job, so he told me he could find one for me while I looked for something better. I started to picture everything we could have, but that dream was shattered. By *him*.

"Olivia, dinner's ready!" Mom's voice drifted from the kitchen. Dinner? Now? I couldn't even swallow my own saliva without choking. The thing about heartbreak is that sometimes you don't know when it's going to hit you. One moment, you are so sure about someone, and the next, everything can end like nothing ever happened.

I dragged myself downstairs, legs heavy, face sticky with the tears that kept coming down my face. The second she saw me, she knew. "Oh, baby girl, what's wrong?" Her arms wrapped around me before I could answer, and I just fell apart. I couldn't hold it anymore. The tears, the pain, all of it spilling out in one ugly flood. And I was drowning in it.

"He dumped me, Mom. He doesn't want me anymore." The words shredded me from the inside out. I was shaking so hard I could barely breathe. My eyes burned, my vision blurred, and my face was so swollen that it didn't feel like mine anymore.

"What happened? Do you want to talk about it?" she whispered, and I swear her voice was so gentle, it felt like she could stitch me back together. But I only shook my head and clung tighter, as if I let go, I'd fall apart completely. "I don't want to eat. I think I'll go for a walk to clear my head."

"Okay, honey. Be careful."

My feet carried me outside before I even thought about it. Straight toward his house. Maybe it was muscle memory or instinct. The same streets I have walked a thousand times, the only difference is that today, each step feels heavier than the last, each turn pressing the sadness deeper.

When I got there, Larna was on the porch, rocking gently on the chair like she had been waiting for me. Maybe she knows. She had the phone in her hand. "Hey, sweet girl. I was about to call you," she said softly, lifting it like proof. My throat closed for a split second. "He's not coming back, is he?" She didn't even have to say it. She just shook her head, and that was it. I broke. The sobs tore out of me. I thought I couldn't cry anymore. I thought I'd run dry. I was so damn wrong.

I knew that was going to be the last time I heard his voice. I know him, and he is not the type of boy who would beg. He never took rushed decisions, so I knew this was the end.

He was really gone.

And we were really over.

CHAPTER ONE
OLIVIA

I GLANCE AT THE CLOCK ON MY NIGHTSTAND — 5:09 a.m. Oh shit, I totally spaced out.

It's mornings like this when everything comes into perspective.

I have so much to do today, and so little time. I need to reschedule all the calls I had for the day. I need to talk to my assistant so she can handle my calendar. I need to postpone an international call with a client I have been dreaming of working with for *months*. Or maybe my assistant can do that. Yeah, she is qualified enough to do so.

Okay, I need to write that down.

I open my computer, start making adjustments, and write down notes as they come to mind. I sent a few emails and closed it out. My flight leaves in about an hour and a half, and I'm about 14 minutes from the airport. That gives me about 45 minutes to finish packing, get there, go through security, and relax before boarding.

Relax, like I know what the hell that word means. Ugh, I should've packed last night.

I grab my phone, ignoring the pile of clothes that I haven't packed yet, and make the call I've been dreading to do since I woke up at 2:05 a.m. this morning, "Hello, how are things holding up?" What else can I ask? I don't know what to say in a moment like this. There are some things they never teach us as kids, such as how to act in difficult moments. I guess it comes with age, maybe.

Once you are an adult, you know that you are supposed to act in a certain way around certain people or conduct yourself in a certain manner around others. But they never teach you how to be there for your parents. Even as a mother, I have no idea how to be there for her.

"Well, all I can say is today has already been hell on earth, and it's barely five in the morning." Julia's voice is calm, a bit sharp, but there's sadness under it. I swallow hard, and my throat goes dry. "We haven't slept all night, and when I say *we*, of course, it's *me*. Mom took some sleeping pills last night, so thankfully, she had a solid 6 hours of sleep. But she has been up since 3:30 a.m.-ish, and since then it's been chaos. The phone hasn't stopped ringing. Her cellphone, my cellphone. It's a mess."

Julia is spiraling, and I don't blame her. This has to be one of the hardest deaths we've ever had to go through. And as always, I'm not there with them.

Larna was my mom's best friend. And she is, *was*, Ethan's mother. The woman who used to braid my hair after school, who I know let me sneak into her house after curfew, just to kiss my boyfriend one last time. She let me cry on her front porch when he left for college, and I stayed behind. And again, when he broke up with me. For good. "I don't even know what to say to mom. What the hell am I supposed to do?"

Julia's voice crackles, "Ask the pilot to come as fast as he can? Meeting the safety standards, obviously," I can hear a faint laugh on her end, and that's more than enough to make me take a breather. I finish tossing what's left of the pile of clothes into my carry-on and zip it shut. "Sure, I'll let him know you said that." A small laugh escapes me. "I'll text you from the airport, okay?" I don't want to go, but I know I have to. "Okay, love you, bye."

Carry on? Check. Bag? Check. The cellphone is fully charged, and the charger is in the bag. The laptop and charger are there. My work phone is also there. I think I'm ready. Key word here, *think*. I'm definitely not.

THE SMELL of cinnamon and steamed oat milk meets me halfway down the stairs. And that's how I know that Beatriz just finished making coffee. I don't know what I'd do without her. She's not just the nanny. She basically runs this house. She's been with us for over five years now. At this point, she is part of the family.

I go into the kitchen and grab my mug to take that first sip of coffee. I let it warm my entire body while I stare at nothing. That first sip in the morning is what gets me going. It's the only moment in the day when I can let my mind go blank. But apparently that's not working today. Because my mind is a mess.

David appears and stands beside me, phone in one hand, pouring coffee with the other into the Father's Day mug the kids painted a couple of years ago. Tiny blue handprints stamped across the ceramic. Our little family frozen in time. It makes me smile, then a bit sad. Larna would've loved those handprints. She always said kids leave their marks whether you want them to or not. She was not wrong at all. But she never met them. A part of me couldn't let that happen, given the history.

"All packed?" David asks, getting me out of my head. "Yeah. I'll finish my coffee and get going." I study him, the way I always do. David is the man everyone admires. He is sharp, smart, charming, put-together, and, God, he is handsome. "Want me to take you to the airport?" His eyes scan me. He knows me better than anyone, and I know he can see I'm struggling, but he won't say anything I'm not ready to say myself.

And for that I'm grateful.

"No, the car's scheduled. But thank you." He nods and leans against the counter. "Where are the boys?" I asked to change the subject. I don't need small talk this morning. "Still upstairs. Beatriz just went up to grab them." And almost on cue, soft footsteps echo down the hall, followed by the thump-thump-thump of Mathew's feet on the stairs.

"Mommy!" he calls, barreling toward me. I crouch to catch him, his little body warm against me, strawberry shampoo still clinging to his hair from last night's bath. "I don't want you to go," he mumbles into my shoulder. "I know, baby." I kiss the crown of his head. "It's just a few days, okay?"

Jeremiah trails after, slower, blanket dragging behind him like always. "You packed your hoodie, right?" he asks. "Of course." I smile, though my chest aches. He's eight going on fourteen, but who am I to blame? He is just like me.

Beatriz appears, bun tight, apron streaked with batter. She gives me a look, maternal, steady, everything I need right now. She always sees more than I show, but she keeps her distance, which I appreciate. "I'll keep them happy and busy. We'll bake cookies tonight. Superheroes, yes?" Mathew brightens. "Even Wolverine?"

"Especially Wolverine."

I run a hand down Jeremiah's back. My throat tightens a bit. I'm not used to being far from my boys, from my home, my family, my routine. David sets his phone down and presses a quick kiss to the corner of my mouth. "Have a safe flight, O. Love you,"

"Love you too." We hug, and Beatriz takes the boys away. I grab my bag and head for the door.

The driver pulls up by the curb. "Good Morning, Olivia. I'll take the bag." He wrestles my suitcase into the trunk, and we are off.

As we pull away, the city blurs, traffic humming, skyline rising and falling. I rest my head against the cool glass. This isn't just me grieving, Larna, it's me grieving my whole life. The one I left in Tacoon, anyway.

THE AIRPORT REEKS of burnt coffee and fuel, which is a horrible mix. I haven't set foot in Tacoon in years. Well, only for holidays or quick trips, but never long enough to feel anything. This time is different, maybe because I'll be there alone. Maybe because I only booked a one-way ticket. Not that I'm planning to stay, God no. But my mom might need me more than she knows right now. And I can't allow whatever I'm feeling or will feel there to make me leave sooner than is needed.

I speed-walk to the gate. The overhead announcements are blurred together. They sound sharp and metallic, each one rattling in my skull. Motion is the only thing keeping me upright. I feel like if I stop, I'll crack. My stomach is in a knot, and I can't seem to loosen up. I feel the acid is crawling up my throat. I make a quick stop at the little market, grab myself a bag of Sour Patch Kids, a Coke Zero— I know I won't drink it, and some gum.

This flight is under two hours, just long enough to sip champagne and pretend I'm cool, calm, and collected.

I board and get to my seat. The plane is almost empty, and there's no one in my row. Not surprised by that, honestly. Nobody flies to Tacoon, let alone at 7:00 a.m. on a random Wednesday.

Once we are at cruising altitude, I stop the flight attendant, "Excuse me, can I get an orange juice and a glass of champagne? Thank you." I expect her to judge my choice, but she just smiles at me. "Do you want that separate, or as a mimosa?"

"Whatever is easier for you," She nods and goes away. Honestly, I could take just the champagne. My hands shake as I take the glass. She hands me a mimosa and an extra bottle of champagne. "On the house," I smiled on the outside, but she clearly saw that I needed the alcohol part of this drink.

Did I say something out loud? Whatever, it doesn't matter. I'll take it anyway.

I pull out my computer and check for any emergencies. But I don't see any. Nothing on my work phone either —just a message on my personal one as we descend.

> Mom: Can't wait to see you. I'll be at baggage claim.

My chest tightens. She must be hurting so bad, and I don't know what to do to make her feel better. Larna has been her best friend since college. They got married the same year and started having kids together. She had Maggie as a newlywed. Everyone used to talk about how she had to be pregnant at the wedding, but only they knew the truth and never told a soul. Then she had Ethan, a year after I was born. Julia and Leo were born a few years after us. We grew up like siblings. We were all really close until Ethan and I fell in love.

I mean, we stayed close for a while. And then, I guess we just grew up.

When the plane lands and the door opens, I can feel the cold November air slapping against my skin. Tacoon doesn't believe in fall. It's like it doesn't get the memo that there's supposed to be a season between summer and fucking winter. Which is rigid here.

The airport is quiet at this time in the morning. And basically, all day. This is a small town, so only a handful of flights arrive and depart each day. I'm lucky I got one on such short notice.

But all that '*luck*' slips away when I see him.

Fuck my life.

CHAPTER TWO
ETHAN

THE THING ABOUT GRIEF? IT DOESN'T WAIT until someone dies.

It creeps in way before that.

Is in the first time they forget your birthday. Or miss a call. Or take too long to text back. It's in the way their laugh gets weaker. That's when it really starts.

By the time the end comes, it's just an echo.

I hadn't cried since the night she passed. I didn't even have time for that. Between the funeral arrangements, the flower orders, and picking between a dark gray or navy casket liner, like that mattered at all. I barely had time to breathe and to come to terms with what just happened.

I just kept moving. Didn't stop long enough to let it hit. At least not until now. I guess flying over there makes everything *real*.

I drop into an empty seat near the gate, and the cold from it goes through my jeans. The airport hums, that low and constant buzz of wheels, chatter, and boarding calls, all of it just blurs together. Someone's kid is crying three gates down. I hear a coffee machine hissing somewhere behind me, as my phone buzzes.

HANNAH

Her face fills the screen. Messy bun, tired eyes, sunlight spilling in through the kitchen window behind her. The one over the sink with the crooked blind that she has told me a thousand times to fix. God, she's beautiful. "Hey," I say, forcing a smile I hope looks real. Although I know I'm not fooling anyone.

"There he is, you left so early I couldn't even say a proper goodbye," she teases, voice soft. "Boarding soon?"

"I know, sorry. Didn't want to wake you all up. They just called the armed forces, so I'll be next." I say as I glance at the crowd. Businessmen with Bluetooths, families wrangling strollers, the usual shuffle. She flips the camera. The girls are on the couch, a blanket fortress around them. "Say bye to Daddy!"

"Bye, Daddy! Love you!" two little voices yell in perfect chaos. I grin like an idiot. "Love you too, girls. Be good to Mom, okay?" They nod, giggling, hair sticking up in every direction. Hannah flips the camera back. "Text me when you land."

"I will. Love you."

"Love you more." The screen goes dark. Just my reflection staring back at my tired eyes. I shove the phone into my pocket as I stand and stretch. My back pops. Coffee. I need coffee.

At the stand, I order a large black coffee and, on

impulse, I grab a bag of Sour Patch Kids. Comfort candy. Always has been, ever since high school. Those bus rides with cracked lips and sugar-dusted fingers were the best. It's funny how certain habits outlive entire versions of us. No matter how much time has passed.

Back at the gate, they're already boarding my group. I toss the candy in my backpack and fall into line. The woman ahead of me smells like lavender and rain. It's a weird combination if you think about it. The guy behind me is muttering about overhead bins. I take a slow sip of the coffee, too hot, too bitter. It's a good distraction.

THE FLIGHT's smoother than I expected. We take off in the rain, the heavy, drumming kind that turns everything outside the window into a smear of silver. The engines roar, the nose tilts up, and the world drops away. Then, we break through. The clouds crack open, and the light pours in. It's bright, the kind that makes you squint even behind sunglasses.

It's always strange, that shift. One minute, you're swallowed by weather; the next, you're above it, flying in perfect calm while the storm keeps raging somewhere below.

I spend most of it with my AirPods in, bouncing between emails and notes for the upcoming site visit. Wi-Fi cuts in and out, but I keep typing like it matters, like keeping myself busy might trick my brain into thinking I'm okay.

A few routine responses:

Got it, thanks.
Will review when I land.
Looks good, just make sure the contractor double-checks the drainage specs.

The usual work language is efficient and safe. Everyone told me to take a few weeks off, but I can't allow myself to do that. I'll drown in my pain, in all the sadness. I'll be taking a few days once I'm in Tacoon, but that's it.

I tweak a few documents and stare at the same spreadsheet for too long. Sip coffee until it's cold and burnt-tasting, the kind that sticks to the back of your throat. The guy next to me is asleep, head back, mouth open. Across the aisle, a woman flips through a book, her thumb tapping rhythmically at the corner of each page.

At some point, I flag down the flight attendant. "Jack and Ginger, please." She smiles politely, pours with practiced ease. I'll have one drink, just one. Just enough to take the edge off. The nerves, the sadness, and everything in between, I don't want to name. It sits warm in my chest as I stare out the window at nothing, at the faint line of the horizon, the endless sky, and wonder why.

The ice clinks. The seatbelt sign dings. Someone laughs two rows up. I close my laptop, lean my head back, and let the hum of the engines fill the space where my thoughts should be.

The plane drops easily, a soft glide through a sheet of low clouds. No turbulence, no bounce, just a smooth surrender to gravity. Wheels kiss the runway, a muffled thud, then that long, rising whine of reverse thrust.

Out the window, Tacoon looks the same as ever. Flat, familiar, quiet in a way that gets under your skin. The fields stretch out, brown and bare this time of year. The kind of landscape that makes you remember being seventeen, driving nowhere with the windows down. My stomach tightens anyway. It always does, right before the door opens. That old, dumb reflex, like bracing for something you can't quite name.

We taxi for what feels like forever. Rows of hangars slide past, a couple of maintenance trucks, the faded tail of some regional airline parked like it's given up. I gather my things: laptop, phone, half-empty coffee cup, and the crinkled bag of Sour Patch Kids from earlier. The flight attendant smiles and says, "Welcome home," without realizing it hits the wrong note.

In the arrivals terminal, the air smells like recently polished floors and too many cinnamon pretzels. The carpet hasn't changed in decades, that ugly blue swirl pattern I used to trace with my shoes as a kid.

I check the board for Leo's flight. It's a little delayed, but nothing out of the ordinary. Ten, maybe fifteen minutes behind. I reach for my phone to text Hannah to let her know I landed.

And I freeze.

For a second, I don't breathe. The noise of the terminal doesn't just fade, it drops away completely. Just the thud of my heart, the echo of footsteps, and that sudden, impossible familiarity that punches through me.

Liv.

She looks the same. Older, yeah. A bit sharper, maybe. The way she holds herself now is guarded, armored up. Her blonde hair pulled back, neutral clothes, face expression I can't read. Not anymore. But the second our eyes lock, something in me snaps back into place.

Sixteen years gone, and still— *it's her*.

I don't smile. I can't. I'm just trying to breathe. She doesn't move either. Just stares at me like I'm a ghost. Maybe I am. Maybe we both are.

Sixteen years. *Sixteen fucking years.*

What the hell am I supposed to say? 'Hey, long time. Sorry, I broke up with you over the phone. Sorry, I ruined everything. Sorry, it took my mom's funeral to get you back here.' But then she steps toward me. Slow, careful, like I'll shatter if she comes too fast. Honestly, I think I might. She stops a few feet away, hands gripping her bag strap like it's keeping her upright.

"Hey." That's it? That's all she's got? "Hey." And as I hear myself saying it back, I realize I sound just as stupid.

"Wow, it's been— I— I just— I wanted to say I'm sorry about your mom, Ethan." I nod. "Thanks, Liv." She's struggling to talk to me. "She was— she meant a lot to me. You know that. Right?"

"I know." God, this is the dumbest conversation

we've ever had. What the fuck is wrong with me? Please fix it. "She talked about you, you know," I say, softer. "Right up until the end." Olivia's eyes shine. Shit, now I'm making her cry. "I wish I had called her more," she whispers. I don't answer. I don't trust myself to. She shifts, glances over her shoulder like she's about to bolt. And then Leo's voice cuts in behind me. "Hey man, I think the car's out front already... Oh, hi, Olivia."

She turns, snapping back into composure. "Hey, Leo." He gives her a half-hug, the kind you do at funerals or, in this case, airports. "I'm so sorry about Larna," she says, looking at both of us. "Thanks," Leo says.

"Well, I should—" She looks past us and spots her mom. "Yeah. I'll see you around. Thanks for being here." I say, softer than I mean to. She offers the smallest smile. "Yeah, sure. See you around, Ethan. Bye, Leo."

I watch her go. Her mom pulls her in, then waves at me. Olivia laughs at something she said. And they walk off arm in arm. She doesn't look back. Not once. And I don't blame her.

Leo nudges me toward the exit. We grab our bags and head for the car. I just realized that

I'm not just grieving my mother, I'm grieving her too.

THE HOUSE SMELLS like lilies and lavender. Dad and Maggie are cleaning around the kitchen. "Oh, my boys, how were the flights?"

"Long," Leo and I say in unison, it sounded like we rehearsed that answer. We all laugh. Finally, a good, real laugh. "Anyone want coffee, tea, alcohol?" Maggie asks, holding up a bottle of whiskey like it's medicine. "Your old man is tired," Dad says, pushing back from the table. "I'm going to bed to rest a bit, but I'll be down for dinner. You kids, have a drink. Just one." He gives a small smile, the kind that doesn't reach his eyes, and disappears down the hall.

"I'll take one," Leo says, nodding at the bottle.

"What the hell, give me one too." I need that drink. Maggie nods, pours three glasses, and sets them on the coffee table. The whiskey stings going down. We sit in silence for a minute, the weight of the house pressing in on us, the flowers, the half-cleaned dishes, Mom's sweater still folded over the arm of her chair.

"She would've hated this," Maggie finally says. Her voice cracks, but she laughs through it. "Us sitting here like some sad movie cliché, drinking Dad's good whiskey."

"She'd be yelling at us to turn on music," I add. "Something loud. Probably Santana."

"Or Gloria Estefan," Leo says, smirking. "God, remember how she used to dance in the kitchen to 'Conga' while cooking arroz con pollo?" We all laugh at the memory.

"She had no rhythm at all," Maggie says, wiping her eyes. "None. But she didn't care."

"She said confidence was half the dance," I say, shaking my head. "The other half was wine."

Leo grins, raising his glass. "To Mom. Worst dancer in the room. Best at everything else." We clink glasses. For a second, it feels like she's here. The silence creeps back in, softer this time. Maggie leans back against the couch. "You know, being the oldest doesn't get easier. I'm still the one who has to keep you, idiots, in line."

"Please," I scoff. "You peaked when you taught me how to sneak out without Dad hearing."

"That was me," Leo cuts in. "I'm the mastermind." Maggie gives him a look. "You were eleven. You couldn't even reach the window lock." I smirk, shaking my head. "Yeah, you were the decoy. The kid who got caught so Maggie and I could get away." Leo groans. "Still bitter about that, thanks." We all laugh again, this time real, and Maggie lifts her glass. "She'd like this. Us together. Laughing. Even if it's through the worst night of our lives."

We raise our glasses again, the three of us clinking them hard enough to echo. "To Mom."

After a while and a couple of whiskey glasses later, I excuse myself and take the path out back to the guest house. The place is small. It's a converted cottage with creaky floors, a kitchen that eats half the space, and a room where the giant bed barely fits. It has a second room that's currently just storage, but it has potential. The most important thing about this place is that it's quiet. The porch opens straight onto the lake. It's the best view in the house.

My phone buzzes as I stare at nothing. *Hannah*. I stare at the screen for a second, then answer. "Hey."

"Hi, love." Her voice is soft, the way it gets when she knows I'm close to the edge. "How was the flight?"

"Long as hell."

"Are you okay?" I close my eyes. "I don't know." She doesn't rush me. Just let the silence hang. She knows better than to try to take the words out of me. "The girls want to say hi," she says. Static, then giggles. "Daddy!" Claire's voice is bright and sweet. "We made a card for Grandma Larna." Leight chimes in. My throat tightens. "That's perfect, baby. She'd love that."

"When are we coming to see you?" Claire asks. "Soon. I'll call before bed, okay?"

"Okay! Love you!"

"Love you more." The phone goes back to Hannah. We sit in the quiet for a few more seconds. I hear pots clanking around the kitchen in the background. Sounds like a normal life. The one I built with the family I love. A wife who's everything to me. And still, all I can think about are those green eyes I haven't seen in sixteen years, and the ache they left behind. "I'll call you in the morning," I say finally.

"Okay. Love you, Ethan."

"Love you too." I set the phone down and stare at the ceiling until it hurts. Because grief isn't always loud, sometimes it's your mother's voice fading. Or the girl who once promised forever walking away.

CHAPTER THREE
OLIVIA

HE LOOKS GOOD, WAY TOO GOOD, AND I HATE that I noticed. But I have eyes, okay?

And unfortunately, a mind that remembers it all too well. I can't believe he still has this power over me.

I swallow the lump in my throat. I don't know what the hell I'm feeling. Maybe it's grief, or nostalgia, or even sadness? It's all tangled up together, and I hate it. And while I hate feeling this way, one thing is painfully clear. My time here is going to be hell. And not only for Larna's death.

As I stare at myself in the mirror, I remember when this room felt huge. Now, it feels like the walls are swallowing me.

The way he said my name, '*Liv*', no one calls me that anymore. I hate how much I loved the way it sounded on his lips. *Fuck Olivia, stop*.

Steam fogs the mirror until my reflection blurs, thank God. I don't want to look at her anymore. That's the girl who has too many memories in this place. The one who still reacts to him like she's sixteen. And that's not me, not anymore.

I step into the shower and let the hot water fall against my shoulders. It's too hot, but I don't move. I want it to burn. Maybe this way I can focus on something else, not this stupid sadness or whatever it is I'm feeling.

After a while, I shut off the water, wrap myself in a towel, and take a deep breath until my hands stop shaking. Good, I'm regaining control over myself.

I get dressed quickly, just some black leggings, a soft, oversized sweater, and I get my hair in a messy bun, the only mess I'm allowing myself to have right now. I almost look steady again. *Almost.*

I have the habit of controlling everything, or at least trying to. And I have to say I'm good at it. Even my feelings. Well, *especially* my feelings. I've always been the '*cold*' one. The one that's always *okay*. That person who you don't need to worry about because you know she'll be fine no matter what. I hate to admit it, and I will *never* say this out loud, but sometimes I get tired of it.

DOWNSTAIRS, the house hums with their slow voices and clinking dishes. Julia's already at the counter, scrolling on her phone, but she looks up when I enter.

Mom— *Mooney to everyone else*— is at the sink, her hands braced on the edge like she's holding herself steady.

She doesn't turn as she talks. "It doesn't feel real." Her voice is low, and it just sounds... painful. "Forty years of friendship, and I keep thinking I should just call her. Tell her some silly story or ask if she wants to meet me at the farmer's market. My hand almost reached for the phone this morning before I remembered." Julia slips off the stool and goes to her, resting a hand on her back. "Oh, Mom..."

Mom shakes her head, blinking hard. "She was supposed to outlive me. We used to joke about that. How she'd be the one holding my hand at the end, bossing everyone around, making sure they got the flowers right." Her laugh cracks halfway through. "And now it's me, planning hers. Do you know how wrong that feels?"

I step closer, sliding in on her other side, my hand finding hers where it clings to the counter. Her skin feels cold, tight. "We know, Mom. But we're here, you don't have to do this alone." Her shoulders drop, but the tears come fast, heavy. Julia wraps an arm around her waist, and I squeeze her hand tighter. For a moment, we hold her, the three of us locked together in the kitchen as we keep her from collapsing.

When she finally speaks, her voice is barely a whisper. "She was my person— the one who knew everything, before your father, before either of you. There's no one left who remembers me at twenty. Or who I was before I became a mom." That lands heavy. I feel Julia press her forehead against Mom's shoulder. "Then we'll remember for you. We'll carry it, too." Mom exhales, a shudder that sounds like release and ache all at once. She squeezes our hands back. "I don't know what I'd do without you girls." And in that moment, it's clear to me, we're not just her daughters tonight. We're the ones keeping her upright. And I need to shut down whatever I'm feeling because even though I'm hurting too, my pain is not the important one.

Dinner was mainly quiet. You could only hear the clinking of the forks, sometimes too loud. When we finished, I stood and started stacking plates. "I got this," I said, nodding toward the sink. Mom just pressed a kiss to my shoulder, too tired to argue, and headed upstairs. I rinsed the last dish under hot water when Julia grabbed an open bottle of wine and two glasses. She didn't say anything, just leaned against the counter until I was done, then walked straight out back. I dried my hands and followed her.

The back porch hasn't changed much.

Same creaky boards, same swinging chairs, same view of the lake that's been our backdrop since we were kids. But there's a new couch tucked against the railing, deep cushions that look a bit out of place here. Julia caught me staring. "Bought it a couple of months ago. I got so sick and tired of the old chairs," she said with a shrug. I chuckled under my breath. "Doesn't surprise me that you wanted to redo the whole place."

We sat side by side, sinking into the cushions. She poured the wine and handed me a glass. Neither of us spoke. We didn't need to.

The lake was still. It looks like black glass stretching out under the moonlight. The air bit our skin. It was way too cold to feel comfortable, but neither of us went inside. We just sat there, drinking, staring at nothing, and letting the silence do the talking. "Well, I just needed that one glass, but you can have the bottle," Julia says, smirking as she stands. "Oh, I will drink this bottle," I tell her, lifting it. She laughs, it sounded a bit hollow, but it was real. "Get some rest. Tomorrow's going to be hell." I nod, watching her disappear inside.

The night settles around me as I pour myself another glass. The wine is colder now, and I stare out at the lake. The water is so still, so peaceful that for a minute, my mind goes quiet.

From here, I can see Ethan's house. The back porch light is on, and the guesthouse windows glow, too. He must be staying there. My chest tightens a bit. Why do I even care? Sixteen years should've been enough to stop looking for him in the dark. I shake the thought away and grab my phone. My thumb hovers before I scroll to Recent Calls and tap on David.

"Hey," David answers on the second ring, his voice low. "Hi," I say, curling tighter into the couch. "Were the kids okay tonight?"

"They were fine. Beatriz made pasta, and apparently, Mathew is now a self-proclaimed Parmesan addict." I can hear the smile in his voice. I laugh softly. "That sounds like him."

"They're both asleep already." My chest warms at the thought. There's a pause, gentle, comfortable. "How's your mom holding up?" I exhale. "Fragile. She tries to keep busy, but... You can see it. The cracks are there. Julia and I are doing what we can, but it's hard seeing her like this."

"I can't even imagine," he says quietly. "And Julia? You two hanging in there?"

"Yeah. We sat outside for a while. She bought this big couch for the porch. Said she was tired of the old chairs." David chuckles, and I smile, staring at the lake. "She's trying. We both are."

"Good," he says, softer now. "And you? How are you holding up?" I hesitate. "I don't know. It feels heavy." He's quiet for a moment, then, "You don't have to carry it all alone, O. Even from home, I'm here for you. Call me if you need me. Call me even if you don't."

My throat tightens a little. "I know. I— I miss you."

"Miss you too," he says. "You'll get through this, okay?"

"Kiss the boys for me."

"Always. Love you."

"Love you too." I end the call and sit in the quiet, staring out at the lake. The cold's gone from sharp to unbearable, so I drain the last of my wine and finally head inside.

After locking up, I climb the stairs to my room, which unfortunately overlooks the lake. The guesthouse light is still burning across the water, a reminder I didn't ask for. I change into pajamas, slide under the covers, and stare at the ceiling for too long. Sleep. I need sleep.

CHAPTER FOUR
ETHAN

The sun is too fucking bright in this guesthouse.

Somebody should've put some curtains up. I stare at the ceiling until my eyes ache, then finally grab my phone.

November 4th, 6:02 a.m. Today is going to be a long and painful day.

The house is quiet, way too quiet. I swing my legs out of bed, feet hitting the cold floor. My chest is already tight, feels like I have no room to breathe. Maybe a shower will take the edge off. The water comes out freezing before it warms, and I let it burn my skin. I brace my hands against the tile and lower my head, steam rising around me. I scrub down fast, not because I'm in a rush, but because I can't stand still long enough to let it all catch up.

By the time I shut off the water, I'm shaking. I towel off and stare at the suit hanging on the chair. Black, somber, pressed, ready, and waiting for me. But I'm not prepared for this. I don't think I'll ever be.

In the kitchen, I make coffee the way Mom liked it, too strong, almost bitter. The smell fills the place, and for a second, it's like she's here. The memory hits harder than I expect, and I have to grip the counter until the sting behind my eyes passes. The coffee burns down my throat as I sip on it and glance out the window. Across the lake, her mom's house sits quiet, except for the faintest shadow moving behind the curtains upstairs.

She's there. And for the first time all morning, my heart doesn't feel like stone. But it feels like it might break all over again.

So, at this point, I don't know which one is worse.

THE CHURCH FEELS TOO small with this many people packed inside. I should be grateful to know that Mom was really loved here. Everyone knew her, everyone wanted to show up. But right now, it just feels suffocating.

"I can't believe they put the fucking lilies in the center. I told them sides only, not the center." Maggie's voice cuts through my thoughts. Her voice is sharp, and she is pissed. Which I'm thankful for, because I needed the distraction.

"Language, young lady. You're in a church, for

Christ's sake," Dad mutters with a half-laugh. He doesn't actually care. He's never been religious a day in his life, but he enjoys giving Maggie shit when he can. She scoffs, heels clicking against the tile as she keeps walking.

Dad lingers beside me. His hand rests on my shoulder, heavy, grounding. "You okay, son?" The question throws me off. If today's brutal for me, it's got to be hell for him. "Yeah... you?" He exhales, eyes on the casket. "I need to be okay. Otherwise, your mother will come back to kick my ass." That gets a laugh out of me. "Yeah. She would." And for a second, standing there with him, it feels like we're both holding each other up.

The service is... fine. Nice, even. People said all the good things they could think of, shared stories, hugs, tears. But Maggie's speech— no one was topping that. She's always had a way of finding the words, of speaking for all of us when we can't. Oldest child privilege, I guess.

Afterward, we go through the motions, shaking hands, hugging neighbors, saying goodbye to those who won't be coming by the house, and saying "see you later" to those who will. "I should get going," Maggie says, already shifting into command mode. "Aunt Davia's coming with me to get the house ready. Catering should be arriving soon." Her voice is steady, clipped, like she's running logistics for work instead of Mom's funeral. We nod.

"Tell Mooney you're leaving," Dad adds, rubbing his temple. "She's got the flower people lined up to deliver everything to the house." That hits me. Mooney means Olivia. Which means later, in the house, I'll have to see her *again*. Here we fucking go. This day keeps getting harder.

We gather our things, shake the priest's hand, and thank him before slipping out. The air outside feels heavy, like even the sky knows what kind of day this is.

THE RIDE HOME is mostly quiet. Dad is mumbling about how many people he hasn't seen since high school, Leo rolling his eyes at the ones who haven't let us breathe since Mom passed. None of it sticks. It's just noise to fill the silence. I stare out the window as I drive, watching the town blur by. When we finally pull into the driveway, the cars are already lining the street and crowding the yard. The windows glow, and through the glass we can see shadows —people moving everywhere, eating, drinking, talking.

As I kill the engine, Dad says, "Alright, boys. Time to be good hosts. Otherwise, your mother will come back to haunt us all." We chuckle, soft and tired, but we know he's right. If anyone could raise hell from the other side over a badly hosted wake, it'd be Mom. We climb out, straighten our jackets, and head inside together.

I'm leaning by the patio doors, whiskey in hand, talking to Leo. Or more like letting him talk while he laughs at his own jokes. I don't laugh. Haven't really had it in me lately. I stare at him and nod. Like I always do.

That's when I spot her, but I act like I didn't see her. *Coward*. And the second she steps out onto the porch, I feel like the ground shifts under me. "Hey, Leo," she says, easy. Chill. Like she didn't just turn my chest inside out. And then her eyes find me.

I turn, and it's like no time has passed at all.

"Hey," I say.

"Hi." Leo glances between us, smirk fading. He knows better. Brother code kicks in quickly. "Going to check on Dad," he says, and slips back inside, which leaves us alone for the first time in sixteen years, that's if you don't count the hundred people on the house.

I take a slow sip of whiskey, nod once. The silence stretches. This is awkward. It feels like even the air remembers what we were, even if we're pretending, we don't. She's the one who breaks it. "So, I won't do the sad questions. How's life outside of this?" She gestures toward the house. I scoff, caught off guard. Of all the things I could've said, I just landed with, "Good." She raises a brow. "Good? That's all I get?"

"Didn't realize we were playing catch-up," I shoot back, but it comes out rougher than I mean. Her eyes don't flinch. "How's married life?" And there it is— a pause I can't cover. Barely a second, but I know she could feel it.

"Good, Hannah's good," I say finally. "Is good your new favorite word?" she shoots back. God. I hate her for making me smile like this. She's still feisty. Still funny. Still *her*.

"Maybe I'm just trying to keep things simple," I say,

swirling the whiskey in my glass. "You know, one-word answers. Low expectations." She tilts her head, lips twitching like she's fighting a grin. "Always the minimalist. Some things never change." She says, rolling her eyes at me.

"Some things do." I don't mean for it to come out so low, but it does. Her eyes flick to mine. For a second, we're teenagers again, arguing about nothing on this same porch until it turned into something. She clears her throat first. "And the kids? You've got two, right?"

"Yeah, two girls. Claire and Leight. You?"

"Two boys. Mathew and Jeremiah. They're loud, but great kids." She smiled at the mentions of them. Good, she's truly happy.

I ask before I can stop myself. "Still living in—?" She cuts me off, "—in the city, yeah." Short answer. Like she's daring me to push further. But I don't. Not yet. I take another sip to see if the burn steadies me. "You always were good at asking questions."

"And you always were bad at answering them." I laugh under my breath, shake my head. "Guess not much has changed after all." Her eyes soften for just a beat. "Guess not."

"What about work?" she asks, like we're doing small talk at a networking event instead of standing on my dad's porch after my mom's funeral. "Busy," I say, keeping it short. "I travel a lot."

"Sounds exhausting." I shrug. "It can be. And you? How's work, life in general?" She chuckles, and it hits me right in the chest because it's the same laugh I remember, just a little older and a bit rougher. "Same. Work is insane. Kids are nonstop. David and I—" She hesitates. Just for a beat. "We've got a good thing going on." I catch it. Of course, I catch it. The pause. The way her voice shifts when she says his name, the way she grips her wineglass.

"So that's us now," she goes on, eyes flicking anywhere but mine. "Two functional grown-ups with solid jobs, families, and all."

"Living the dream," I say, dry as hell.

"It's weird, isn't it?" She looks at me with curiosity in her eyes. "What is?"

"This," She gestures between us. "Us talking, being here. It feels like I walked into someone else's life." I nod slowly. "Yeah. I get that." And I do. Standing here with her feels like my whole life tilted sideways, like I'm looking at a split screen, what is, and what could've been.

Something softens in her face, and for once, I don't stop myself. "You look good, Liv," And it comes out way too honest. Her eyes meet mine, and I feel it, that pull I've been pretending doesn't exist. Sixteen years passed, and it's still there. They were simple words, but they landed heavily on her. She smiles, just barely. "Was wondering how long it'd take you to say something like that." I let out a breath of a laugh. "Still impatient, guess you haven't changed that much either."

I let my eyes drag over her, slower this time. I shouldn't, but I do. "But you look steadier, though. Like you're not trying so hard anymore." Her brow lifts. "Wow. Compliment and insult in one sentence. Thanks,

Ethan." I grin, heat sparking low in my chest. "Didn't say it was a bad thing."

"No, but it sure sounded like it." Her voice is sharper than her smile, and it knocks something loose in me. God, I'd forgotten how much I loved this. Her fire, her bite. The sound that slips out of me is a laugh I haven't heard from myself in years. It's too warm, too comfortable.

I hate that she still makes me feel this way, but I also loved that about her.

She doesn't move. Neither do I. Her eyes soften, and they drop just a little. "You look good, too." That stops me cold. My grin fades slowly. My chest tightens like a fist. "Yeah?" Is she flirting with me, or is she just being nice?

"Yeah." Her voice dips lower. "You look like you belong somewhere. Like life fits now." Her words cut deep, sharper than she knows. I want to tell her she's wrong, that nothing has fit right since the day I lost her. Instead, I laugh, "Guess that's what getting older does."

"Guess so." Then it happens— that beat, that shift. The kind that changes everything without a word. She's closer than I realized. Close enough that I can smell the wine on her breath, the faint sweetness of her shampoo. Underneath it, she must catch the whiskey on mine, the cologne she used to fall asleep against. The air between us hums. My pulse kicks. Her eyes hold mine, that green pulling me like they always have. My body leans forward before my brain can catch up. And she doesn't move back.

For one wild second, it feels inevitable. Like sixteen years never happened, like this was always waiting for us. Heat rolls through me, heavy, hungry, and I don't remember the last time I wanted anything this bad. I want to kiss her, to grab her in my arms and tell her everything I haven't for the past almost two decades. Then it shatters, someone inside laughs too loudly, my name carries across the room, and the spell breaks.

I blink, jerk back a step, my throat goes dry. "Well, I should—"

"Yeah. Of course." We retreat, careful, like we just touched fire but are pretending we didn't get burned. She smiles, turns, and walks away. My heart is pounding, pulse racing, like I just ran a mile. I should let her go. Hell, I *have* to let her go. But the words slip out anyway, low, before I can reel them back in. "Liv."

She freezes and turns slowly. And there it is. In her face, her eyes, all that history slamming into me like it never left. My mouth curves into something that feels too close to a smile. "Still dangerous," I tell her. It's the truth. She always was, and she always will be.

She holds my stare, and then God help me, because when she smiles at me, that's it.

That's enough to gut me. And then, she walks away.

CHAPTER FIVE
OLIVIA

THANK GOD THIS EVENING IS FINALLY OVER.

I can't take being in the same room as him one second longer.

That stare. Those eyes. Those *brown eyes*. The way he was looking at me, at my lips, at my body. Nope. Nope. Stop it, Olivia. He wasn't looking at anything. You're making shit up. You have a husband. Two kids. He has a wife. Two kids. A whole damn family.

A perfect wife, by the way. Not that I didn't know that already. I stalked her Instagram seven years ago. And again, five years ago. And, for fuck's sake, a week ago. Blonde-ish, green eyes, sweet smile. Of course. He picked someone who looks just like me. Like I wasn't enough for him, but the idea of me was. And the worst part? I still care enough to notice, to compare us. To hate that it still stings me that she gets to have a life with him. Ugh!

I press my palms against my eyes, like I can block him out, erase the way my body lit up under his gaze. But it's useless. Because I know the truth, I can't say it out loud, but I know it. Sixteen years later, Ethan Cole is still the most dangerous man in the room. And he dares to say I'm the dangerous one.

THE HOUSE IS QUIETER. Even the walls feel like they're exhaling after all the chaos from today. Mom, Dad, and Anne are in the kitchen, voices low, talking about the service. I pause in the doorway, watching them. The three of them move around each other so easily that it almost looks normal. I'll never understand it. But I guess I don't have to.

I couldn't imagine divorcing my husband because he cheated, watching him marry his mistress, and then opening the door to both of them as if nothing had happened. But my mom? She does it with grace. A saint, really. Julia's beside me, rolling her eyes the second Anne laughs at something Dad says. I can't help but laugh. "Quit it, Jules."

"I just don't get it," she mutters. "We don't have to," I say. "If it works for them, that's enough for me." She shoots me a look. "Yeah, because you didn't have to grow up with her."

Ouch. That one stings. She's not wrong. When I left, I left her behind. Both of them. God knows it still hurts to admit it, but I couldn't stay here, not after everything.

I exhale, "I know. I shouldn't talk about something I didn't live. But... she's nice to Mom. She makes Dad happy. And sometimes in marriages, in relationships in general, that's what it comes down to." Julia huffs, crosses her arms. "I hate you."

I bump her shoulder. "No, you don't." Her mouth twitches, then she nods, smiling in spite of herself. She knows I'm right. "You want a glass of wine?" I offer. She shakes her head. "You know what, I'm calling it. I'm exhausted."

"You must be if you're turning down wine." We both chuckle, the tension breaking for now. I watch her head down the hall before I climb the stairs, the house too loud and too quiet all at once. I drag myself upstairs, slow, heavy, like my body's fighting me. Change into an old sleep shirt and underwear, tug my hair down, and crawl into bed.

Sleep? Yeah, right. Not happening.

'*Still dangerous.*' The way Ethan said it, it's on a loop in my head. I need to get him out of here. I grab my phone and call David. His voice is steady and reliable, as always. We talk about the kids, dinner, bedtime, and some juice spilled on the couch— the usual stuff. I clutch it like a lifeline, as if I anchor myself in routine, I'll be alright. But when we hang up, the quiet swallows me. And Ethan's still there. In my head. Under my skin. *Fuck*.

I stare at the ceiling, one hand under the pillow. The other knows exactly what it wants. I reach into my bag, pull out the vibrator I packed like the good, responsible adult I pretend to be. Just in case I needed help falling asleep.

I lie back, press it between my legs, and even before I switch it on, I know where my mind's already going— no fantasy needed. I think about his hands, his mouth. That look in his eyes earlier, hungry but restrained, like he wanted me and hated himself for it. I close my eyes and let myself go.

That low rasp of my name in his voice. The way he used to say it was like I wasn't just someone, I was *his* someone. My nipples tighten under my shirt as I roll one between my fingers. My body responds instantly. My hips are shifting, chasing the pressure. My thighs fall open. Breath shaky, spilling out too fast.

I picture him over me, mouth on my neck, his hands gripping my waist. That sound he made right before he lost control. The rhythm builds, faster, harder. My body arches, grinding into the toy, chasing it, needing it. His voice in my head, my name breaking me apart.

The orgasm rips through me, sharp and deep. My back arches, breath stuttering out silently. Tight, then loose, leaving me raw, empty, and wrecked. I blink at the ceiling, chest heaving, skin damp. And it hits me, cold and brutal.

I didn't think about David.

Not once.

Shit.

THE MORNING COMES QUIETLY, just a ray of sunshine creeping through the window. I glance at my cellphone, which I forgot to charge last night, with all the *distractions*. It's almost ten in the morning. I haven't slept this much since before becoming a mother—shit, even before owning a company—so that's nearly ten years.

The smell of coffee drifts up the stairs, rich and warm. I want it like oxygen. Even as I brush my teeth and wash my face, he's there. Ethan. His eyes. That stare.

This is hell, being back here, carrying him like a ghost in my head.

I grab my laptop, my phones, both chargers, and head downstairs. "Good morning, Olivia." I stop short. Anne. She's at the counter, bright smile in place, handing me a mug. Did she spend the night? Weird. "Morning, Anne. Didn't expect to see you here."

"Oh, I decided to come early to help your mom with breakfast. I didn't want her to be alone today." I bite my tongue. She's not alone. Julia and I are here. But sure, Anne. "How thoughtful of you," I say, forcing a smile. She beams and passes me a coffee. Damn it. It smells amazing.

Julia wanders in a minute later with bed hair and a raised eyebrow, shooting me a *what the fuck is going on?*

Look. I shake my head. Anne does the same routine, hands her a mug, then breezes out to the porch where Mom and Dad are talking. "This is hell," Julia mutters. She's not wrong. I laugh and open my computer to see if I can get some work done. And when I turn on my work phone, all the messages and voicemails come buzzing. "Oh fuck" Julia leans closer. "Everything okay?"

"Yeah, just work piling up. I need to get through this."

"Yeah, sure. You want to go grab brunch downtown later?"

"That sounds amazing, give me one hour," She just nods, and goes my way to try and calm the chaos. The thing about work is that I'm the boss, but I'm also an employee because, of course, no one does things the way I want to, so I end up doing it myself.

In this field, presence is everything. When you work with small businesses or even big companies, if you don't have a strong presence, you are out of the game. And I can't be out of anything.

This year so far, my company has made over 4.2 million dollars, which in any other industry might not seem like a lot, but in the Marketing industry and for a 'small agency' like the papers like to call us. It is.

CHAPTER SIX
ETHAN

THE BUZZ OF MY PHONE YANKS ME AWAKE. I roll over, squint at the screen— two missed calls from Hannah. I sit up, rub my face, and call her right back. She picks up on the second ring. She sounds like she is already halfway through her day, and it's barely 10 a.m., at least here. Which is what, 8 a.m. over there? She should be waking up, not this awake. "Hey, love," she says. The cold floor under my feet jolts me as I stand. "Did I wake you up, honey?"

"No, no. Already up." I don't know why I lied. "You didn't call last night. Figured you passed out, and I didn't want to add more stress to your day. How are you holding up?" I glance at the mirror. Jaw tight. Eyes shadowed. I look exactly how I feel. Sad, tired, mad, and all the terrible feelings in the world.

"Yesterday was hard," I say, keeping it simple. "But I'm glad it's over." Which is true. "Oh, honey. I can imagine. I wish I were there with you." And I know she does.

But it's better this way. I didn't want the girls to have this memory of their grandmother, to put them through this pain that they don't understand just yet. And although that's the truth, a small part of me didn't want to be a son, brother, husband, and dad while dealing with this grief. So, I decided to be a son and a brother. Maybe it's selfish, but honestly, I don't care.

I don't need more pain than I can carry, and I don't need them to carry a pain they don't deserve.

"I know, love. Don't sweat it." There's laughter and chaos in the background, and God, I miss those little brats. One of them is yelling about socks, probably Claire. "They wanted to say hi." A text pings. When I check it, it's a picture of her and the girls, still in their pjs, Claire mid-scream, Leight grinning like a tiny maniac. "They look happy," I say, staring too long. "They miss you."

"I miss them too." And of course, I do. "We'll call later?"

"Please do."

"I love you, Ethan."

"I love you too." The line goes dead, and I stare at the screen. This is my life, my family, the one I built. So why the fuck did I spend all night thinking about someone else?

I step into the shower and crank the heat until the room fills with steam. Press my palms flat against the tile, head down. Olivia's in my head like she never left. Like I never left her.

The way she said my name. It's still fucking echoing.

I try to shake it, but it creeps back in. The memory of her mouth on mine, that sound she made when I used to kiss just below her jaw. I groan. My hand drops without hesitation. Guilt sparks, but it doesn't stop me. I stroke slowly at first, like it's a warm-up. But the image of her sharpens everything. Her thighs around my waist. Her nails are dragging down my back. My pace quickens, my hips tense. My breath is ragged. If she were here, I know she'd feel even better.

Fuck.

I came hard and fast. A full-body thing that rips through me and leaves me sagging against the tile, chest heaving. Steam clings to me like the guilt I wish I could wash off. I rinse off like I'm trying to erase it. But it doesn't go anywhere.

She doesn't go away.

BY THE TIME I make it up to the main house, Dad and Leo are in the living room, both nursing half-drunk coffees. Maggie's curled in the armchair, legs tucked under her, a folder in her lap. Papers are spread across the table and counter like the aftermath of a storm.

"Morning," I say. Maggie glances up and gives me a soft smile. "Morning, sleepyhead. We were waiting for you."

"For me? What did I do?" I ask, honestly confused. I

see a mess of paperwork. "Nothing," Dad says, voice low, steady. "We're just gathering the documents for your mother's will." He says it like it's obvious, like I should've known already. Maybe they told me, and I forgot. Or maybe I just blocked it out. Maggie doesn't look up again, flipping through papers with one hand, holding her coffee with the other.

"The reading's today. We need to be there around two-ish." I nod and head to the kitchen. I need coffee first, then I'll deal with the rest. "Wanna go grab breakfast? I'm starving. And Maggie said she's not cooking for us. She only made breakfast for Dad," Leo says, knowing damn well it'll piss her off.

"I didn't say that," Maggie shoots back immediately, straightening the stack of papers like she might throw one at him. "I said that I already made breakfast at seven a.m. It's almost ten. I'm not going back in the kitchen for you guys." I chuckle into my coffee. Same fight, different day. Those two could bicker through the apocalypse. "Yeah, let's go grab something," I say, setting the mug down. "You coming, Maggs?" She sighs as if she's being dragged, but stands anyway. "Of course. But you're paying." I shake my head. "Yeah, I figured."

DOWNTOWN, the diner looks the same as it always has — neon sign buzzing, front windows fogged from too much bacon grease, and let's be honest, insufficient ventilation. It's one of those places that's been here forever, where you don't even need a menu to know what you'll order.

We push through the door, the smell of coffee and syrup hitting instantly. The hostess looks up, ready with a polite smile, but I get distracted when I see Olivia with Julia waiting for a booth. Maggie spots them, too, and her whole face softens. She steps forward first, smiling widely. "Oh, my God. Olivia, Julia."

Julia stands, polite but reserved. Olivia hesitates a half-beat before rising. "I'm so sorry I didn't get more time with you yesterday," Maggie says, pulling Olivia into a hug. "Everything was... chaos." Olivia nods, hugs her back. They hold on a second longer than usual, and I remember why those two used to be inseparable. Best friends before everything else got in the way. "We'll make up for it," Maggie says firmly, pulling back with glassy eyes.

"Actually," I say, glancing at her and walking towards the hostess, "Can we get a table for five?" Olivia hears me but doesn't look my way. And that's fine by me, I know she is trying to be polite and distant. And hell, I don't blame her. I broke her heart, and we haven't seen each other or talked in over sixteen years. I can't expect anything more from her.

Leo claps his hands together. "Alright, let's eat before I die." Thank God he did, because I was starting down my rabbit hole of guilt. The hostess clears her throat. "Come this way."

"Thanks," I say again, though my voice comes out lower, rougher. My pulse is ridiculously fast right now. And as we follow her toward the table, I can feel Olivia's presence, and that's when it comes back to me. This was the diner where she used to work, and it feels like a lifetime ago, but so recent at the same time. I can't help but laugh at the memory of all the days I spent here.

I shake the thought away when I look at her. She is wearing a tight long skirt, a sweater, and black boots. Her honey blonde hair is up in a messy bun, and she looks put together— nothing like the reckless girl I used to know.

We talk about everything and nothing at all. Julia is talking about her master's, Maggie mentions something about work, and Leo is giving her shit for it. But my attention keeps drifting to her. Olivia leans in to show Maggie a picture on her phone, her family. Husband and kids. She smiles when she talks about them, but it hits me like a sucker punch. I bite my tongue before I say something stupid.

And then she catches me. Her eyes cut across the table, steady, sharp, right through me. Damn it. She can still read me like no one else. She sets her coffee mug down. "Well, it's almost two, we should get going, we have a—" Maggie cuts in, oblivious. "Oh, you're going with Mooney to Mom's will reading, right?"

Silence drops over the table. My chest tightens. Is she going? Olivia nods. "Yeah, my mom asked us to come with her. I'll call her so she can pick us up." She says it casually, but her eyes flick to me, like she's daring me to hear it another way. Like she's making an excuse. I want to believe it. I need to. So, I nod.

"Oh, nonsense," Maggie waves it off. "Come with us. We'll be a little tight, but we'll fit." Oh, I want to strangle her.

In the parking lot, Julia calls shotgun before we even reach the car, sprinting to the front seat. "Hey, not fair," Leo protests, but she's already buckled in, smirking. "Want to drive, Ethan?" Maggie asks. I shake my head. "Nah. I'll sit in the back." And I swear I can feel Olivia rolling her eyes. I pull open the door and gesture. "After you, Liv." She doesn't even look at me. She just slides into the middle seat. Now we're packed shoulder to shoulder, thigh to thigh. Too damn close. I rest my hand on my knee, and my pinky brushes hers. Barely a touch, but she stiffens instantly, spine straight, breath sharp.

The drive is only five minutes, but it feels like hours. I can hear her breathing harder, like she's counting the seconds until she can get out. And the second Leo pushes the door open, she bolts. I don't think, I reach out, catch her hand. "Liv—"

She turns, eyes blazing. "What?" Her voice is tight, sharp, but she's looking at me like she's waiting. Like she'd listen if I actually said it. I freeze, my mouth goes dry, and what comes out is pathetic. "Your bag. Don't forget it." Her lips press together. "Oh yeah, thanks." She pulls away, gone before I can even blink.

And I sit there, hating myself.

What the fuck is wrong with me?

THE WILL READING starts the way I figured it would. Quiet and predictable. Mom left Mooney the greenhouse. No shock there. That place was theirs, fifteen years of sweat and love poured into every plant. They made it magical.

Dad gets the house. We knew that too. "Well, kiddos," Dad says, "your mom and I talked about this. When I'm gone, the house will go to Maggie." He says it like it's news, but it isn't. We all know about that. Maggie's the favorite. She's the oldest, the only one who lives nearby— it makes sense. "I'll rent you guys your rooms," Maggie jokes. "Ethan, you can take the guest house."

We laugh for about two seconds. The attorney clears his throat. "There's something else. Larna had property here in Tacoon." She what? Dad leans forward. "What do you mean she had property?"

"They were passed down from her late father. Technically, not in her name, but written into his will that her children would inherit. She adjusted some things."

My stomach knots. "What kind of adjustments did she make?"

"Maggie, 20%. Leo, 20%. Ethan, 40%." And just like that, the air shifts. Maggie's head snaps up. "Who has the other 20%?" The attorney hesitates. "Josh and Audrey. Ten percent each." Oh fuck!

"Our stepbrothers?" Maggie's voice cuts like glass. "Those bastards?" she spits, straight at Dad. "Hey," Leo says quickly, trying to calm her. "Don't do that, Dad didn't know."

"I didn't," Dad says, stunned. "Maggie, I had no clue." The attorney keeps talking. "They don't know yet. Larna wanted you to hear first."

"Of course she did," Maggie mutters.

"Maggie, enough," I say, sharper than I meant. It lands hard. She glares at me. "Easy for you to say. You got the biggest share."

"Children enough," Dad snaps, tired. "Ralph, please continue." And just when I think it can't get worse— "Larna left a letter and a box. For Olivia."

We all turn. She's on her phone, half-distracted, until the attorney hands them over. Her hand trembles as she tucks them into her bag. Her mom rests a hand on her back. I can't stop staring. A letter makes sense. She was close to Mom. But the box? What the fuck could be in that box? The size is strange. It's not big enough to be a present per se, but not small enough to be a key or a piece of jewelry. "Another secret," Maggie mutters. The attorney continues reading and discussing some technicalities, but I'm not listening.

Olivia's phone buzzes. She rises. "I'm sorry, I need to take this." And then steps out of the office. Ten seconds later, so do I.

She's on the back of the hallway next to the back

door, pacing, voice sharp. "No, Gloria, I told you what to say. Don't fuck this up. Go back inside and fix it." She turns when she hears me, and for a second, just a second, everything around us goes still. Her phone's pressed to her ear, her voice mid-sentence, but the second our eyes meet, she freezes. Whatever she was saying dies in her throat. A tiny flick of her thumb, and the call ends. "Everything okay?" I ask. My voice comes out lower than I intended.

She lets out this laugh, if you can even call it that. It's brittle, nervous, the kind that hides something heavier underneath. "Yeah. Work's a mess."

"Any work is always a mess," I say, because it's the safest thing to say. Still, I can't help the small chuckle that follows. My way of easing the moment or pretending I can. I step closer. Not close enough to touch her, but close enough to feel it, that faint shift in the air, that static. She leans back against the railing, crossing her arms like a shield. The wind lifts a few strands of her hair, and I have the sudden, ridiculous urge to tuck them behind her ear. "You didn't have to follow me." She says, leaning on the railing.

"I know." But I did anyway. I'd seen her walk out, seen that flash of her shoulders tightening the way they always do when she's trying to hold it together. And something in me, an old habit, a bad instinct, made me do it.

Her eyes flick to mine, cautious, curious. There it is again, *the pull*. That quiet gravity that's been screwing with me since the first time I met her. "You look like you want to say something," she says softly. "I do." My jaw tightens. I drag a hand across the back of my neck, trying to find words that won't make things worse. "But I shouldn't."

She tilts her head, the corner of her mouth twitching — half challenge, half defense. "Try me." My eyes drop to her mouth before I can stop them. *Fuck*. Those lips. They were the death of me once. The soft that ruins a man's sense of direction. And for some reason, some stupid, masochistic reason, they still are.

I swallow, jaw tight. "I want to kiss you."

Her breath catches, that small, broken sound that hits harder than it should. "Ethan—"

"I told you, I shouldn't say anything." Her mouth opens like she wants to answer, but the words don't come. Instead, she straightens, crossing her arms again, a wall made of nerves and denial. "You can't do that," she says finally, but it's barely a whisper. A plea more than a command. "I know." I should stop. I should walk away and pretend I didn't just throw gasoline on everything we've been pretending to keep under control. But I don't move. My body doesn't listen. It never does around her.

I take a step closer. Close enough to feel her breath hitch, to see the tiny pulse at her throat. My heart's hammering like I'm eighteen again and making all the same mistakes. "The other night," she says quietly, eyes flicking to mine and then away, "the way we talked... it felt like we crossed a line." She gestures between us, this invisible, electric space we've been orbiting for days.

"This— this has to stop." Her voice cracks just a little on stop, like she doesn't quite believe it herself.

"I know," I say again. It's the only thing I can say that doesn't betray how much I don't mean it. She stares at me, jaw tight, eyes shining with something I can't understand. For a heartbeat, neither of us moves. "You've got a wife. Kids. A family." Her words slice clean through the haze. "And you've got a husband and kids." My voice comes out rougher than I mean it to. "Are we just trading facts now?"

She shakes her head, "I'm just trying to stop this before it turns into something." I swallow hard, and my throat feels dry. "I think we passed that already, Liv." The way she flinches at her own name, like hearing it from me is too much, tells me I'm right. I need to stop. *She* needs to stop *me* before I do something I can't take back.

"No, we haven't, Ethan." Her tone wobbles, trying for firm and missing by an inch. "This is just a memory." Just a memory, my ass. My heart's beating like it didn't get that memo. But her hands are trembling, fingers twisting in the edge of her sleeve, and something inside me slips. I move closer— just a fraction, just enough to feel the heat off her skin. Because apparently, I've lost my mind. "You don't believe that," I murmur. Her eyes flick to mine, wide and unsteady. "You're standing too close."

"You haven't moved back." Her lips part. That tiny breath she takes burns straight through me. "Don't." The word's a whisper, fragile as glass. "I'm not doing anything," I lie, because standing this close is already too much. My fingers brush her arm, light, almost accidental, and she gasps. "You just touched me."

"And you still haven't moved away." She does then, half a step back until her shoulders meet the wall. I follow without meaning to, hands braced on either side of her, caging her in. Her breath catches. Mine matches it. She is nervous.

"When I said that you're still dangerous, Olivia. I mean it," I say quietly. The truth sits between us, heavy and alive. I shouldn't kiss her. God, I know I shouldn't. This will fuck everything up. But she's looking up at me like she remembers exactly how it felt the last time, and that memory is its own kind of gravity pulling me closer to her. I tell myself I need to know, I need to see if she'll stop me. And then I lean in, slow enough to give her every chance to pull away.

She doesn't. So, I kiss her.

The kiss hits like a fuse, the heat, the confusion, all the time we've spent pretending this wasn't inevitable. It's rough, hungry, the kind that burns through good sense before you can remember why you had it.

Her hands clutch at me, nails digging into me through fabric, pulling me closer instead of pushing me off. I can taste everything we shouldn't be. My hands are all over the place, on her waist, her thigh, her hair. She gasps, and I can't stop. *Fuck I don't want to stop.*

I press her back against the wall, not hard, but just enough to feel her heartbeat against mine. The sound of it is chaos. Her legs shift, parting slightly, just enough for me. If I could, I would pull her skirt up and touch her. I bet she is wet right now. No, Ethan, don't. Instead, my mouth finds her neck, and she moans.

Then, somewhere down the hall, voices. A door creaks.

"Fuck." We break apart, gasping like we just surfaced from underwater. Her hand is still clenched in my shirt, my palms still on her body, and for a heartbeat, neither of us moves. We stare at each other.

She looks wrecked, lips swollen, eyes wide with the kind of panic that only comes after wanting something you know you shouldn't. I'm not any better.

She smooths her skirt down with shaking hands, pushes her hair behind her ear, and forces her breathing to slow. She finally looks up at me, and everything in that look says we can't do this again, but also that we might. Then she turns and starts walking toward the office, back straight, every step precise, as if nothing had happened.

I follow her anyway, because I don't know what else I could do. And we definitely should head back inside.

BACK INSIDE, the office felt too warm. Or maybe it was just me. The attorney was stacking the final documents, neat and efficient, like he'd done this a thousand times and never once noticed the lives being rearranged in front of him.

"Now that everything is signed," he said, tapping the

stack into order, "we'll need five to seven business days for the paperwork to process before we can close everything." A collective groan rippled around the room. Chairs creaked, shoulders slumped, grown adults suddenly looking like scolded kids whose recess just got canceled. Leo made a joke about bureaucracy. No one laughed except him.

Olivia sat across the table, perfectly composed. You'd never guess what had just happened out in the hallway. But I could still feel her everywhere. The warmth of her skin was in my palms. The taste of her still haunted the back of my throat.

"Will you be staying?" I asked quietly, leaning just close enough for her to hear. She didn't look at me. "If my mom needs me to, then yes," she whispered. Her tone was steady, but the edge in it gave her away. "I hope she does," I said before I could stop myself. That earned the smallest reaction, a laugh, soft and breathy, half disbelief, half something else. She tried to hide it, but I saw it.

The attorney looked up briefly, then back to his papers. No one else noticed a thing. But between us, it was loud, that invisible current we kept pretending not to feel. She straightened the corner of the file in front of her, a slight, deliberate movement, and said under her breath, "We shouldn't want this."

"I know," I said, eyes on the table, pulse still unsteady. "But I do, and I think you do too."

CHAPTER SEVEN
OLIVIA

THE DOOR CLICKS SHUT BEHIND ME.

The house feels quieter, which is exactly what I need right now. Stillness.

I slip off my boots, walk down the hallway, and head upstairs to my room. My skin still tingles. My lips still burn. The taste of him, the heat, that *need* that hasn't faded. What the hell am I doing?

I sit on the edge of the bed, elbows on knees, and my face in my hands. I can still see it all in my head. I didn't just let him kiss me. I let him *devour* me. I wanted him to kiss me, God help me, I still want it.

But what terrifies me the most is that I don't feel sorry. I don't feel guilty at all. I know I shouldn't be doing this, but I haven't felt him in so long, and I feel like my body needs him. I *should* feel guilty, remorseful, or regretful. But instead, I feel like I've woken up. Like something inside me that's been dormant for years cracked open, and now it won't close.

I strip out of my clothes one layer at a time. The blouse clings to my body like a memory. The skirt feels too tight, too much. I toss them both into the laundry basket and step into the bathroom, turning the water hot enough to burn me alive.

This shower should calm me, but it doesn't. All I can see in my mind is the way he looked at me right before he kissed me. Like he'd been holding his breath for years. Like I was something he'd lost and finally found again.

Somewhere inside me, beneath all the layers of motherhood, marriage, and pretending... I'm still *his*.

I finish the shower quickly, wrap myself in a towel, and move through the nighttime routine. As I finish getting dressed, I hear the phone buzzing. David. I consider letting it go to voicemail. I don't feel like I can face him right now. His voice will be too much, and that's when I realize that I am, in fact, feeling guilty.

I can't do that, I can't avoid what I'm feeling, and he is my husband, for fucks sake, I can't ignore him either. "Hey."

"Hey, love, you home already? How was the reading?" This is good, this is just an everyday, casual conversation with my husband. "Yeah, just got out of the shower. It went fine. There were some unexpected things, but it was like any other attorney meeting."

"Okay, okay." A pause. "Will you be staying there for a while, or when are you thinking of coming back? I don't want to pressure you, it's just that a quick trip that just came up at work, and I need to know how to organize things here."

I rub at my temple. "I honestly don't know yet. Can we talk about this later? There's some paperwork that needs to be done, and I'm sure my mom will need me here for a couple more days."

"Sure, okay. I'm heading into dinner with a few execs, so I can't talk too much right now anyway." Then, faintly, I could hear a female laugh in the background. I know his coworkers and the people he usually dines with. There are no women in that group. My body goes still, but I shouldn't push it. I'm in no place to be the jealous wife right now. But I do it anyway. "Is there someone else with you?" He hesitates. "Just the team. We're at the hotel restaurant." I don't push. But I damn sure know that's a lie. But again, I need to let it go. "Right." I stay silent. "Well. I've got to go."

"Okay. Talk tomorrow."

"Sure. Love you, Olivia," I hang up and stare at the screen. It's not just the kiss with Ethan what's unraveling me right now. It's everything. David. This house. My life. The version of me I keep pretending still fits everywhere, when in reality, I feel like I'm losing myself.

I don't want to feel like this anymore.

When I go to check on my mom, she is already asleep. My dad and Anne are in the kitchen, and I know they won't leave her alone tonight. So, I went and knocked on Jule's door. "Wanna go out tonight?" She looks up, surprised. "You? Out? Where's my sister?" She says, twisting her head, exanimating me. "Ha, ha, ha, funny." I roll my eyes at her.

"I need to decompress, and I don't want to do it next

to Dad and Anne," She grins. "Point taken. Let's go." We get ready between rooms. I didn't pack anything for this occasion, so I went through Julia's closet, which, let's say, has a very different taste than I do. Even though it's freezing out there, I settle for a mini skirt and a blouse that leaves very little to the imagination, but I'll have my coat on, and I pair it with some knee-high boots. That will cover what the outfit doesn't.

WE HEAD TO MIKE'S. A little bar downtown that somehow refuses to die. The place hasn't changed at all. Not even a little. The same flickering neon signs still buzz outside, trying their best to spell out Coors Light but giving up halfway through. This place has never exactly screamed 'welcoming bar'. It has always seemed more like a possible tetanus situation.

Inside, it smells like spilled beer, fryer grease, and a thousand bad decisions. The floor's still sticky —*visibly sticky*— which feels like some kind of health code violation, but also, you know... home.

The same crooked pool table squats in the corner, looking like it's survived some wars. A group of college kids around it, all loud laughter and cheap perfume, taking selfies like they discovered dive bars themselves. Bless their hearts.

I catch our reflection in the mirror behind the bar,

and for half a second, I stare at myself and realize that I look older than I remember. The lighting here is brutal. Murderous, really. I make a mental note never to stand under a Miller Lite sign again.

The bartender looks up and grins, wiping his hands on a towel that's definitely not clean. "Well, I'll be damned. Olivia."

"Mike," I say, smiling despite feeling like absolute shit tonight. "Still here, huh?" He chuckles. "Somebody's gotta keep this dump running."

"Clearly, no one else volunteered," I shoot back, sliding onto a stool. "What's it been? Ten years?" He squints, laughing and pretending to count. "Eight, maybe? You look good. Different, but good." The last time I stepped foot in this bar was before I got pregnant with my eldest. It was the last time David and I came to town. I remember it was just around the Holidays.

"Different but good, huh? So basically, I aged like a person who now works and pays taxes?" I say, flipping my hair back. He laughs, sets down a napkin like it's a peace offering. "What'll it be?"

We order drinks. I go with a bourbon, neat, with a lime wedge tossed in because I like pretending that somehow that makes it lighter. Truth is, I don't even drink bourbon. At home, it's wine —*always wine*— something dry and respectable that matches my glassware and my carefully curated Spotify playlists. At work events, it's champagne. Because bubbles say 'I have it all together' even when I don't.

But tonight? Tonight, I'm not that Olivia. Julia's

already halfway through her vodka soda when she nudges me. "Do you want to do a shot?"

"Nope." She gives me that look, the one that says she's about to make it her personal mission to corrupt me. "Come on. Just one. Pretty please?" I roll my eyes, but she's impossible to resist. Always has been. "Fine. Just one." The other bartender is already reaching for the tequila, lining up glasses with the kind of muscle memory only a man who's seen too much can manage. He's mid-pour when a voice slides in behind me, smooth, low, and completely out of my nightmares.

"Make that four," I swear that every nerve in my body snaps to attention. I don't turn. I honestly don't even have to. The air shifts, and I feel that particular change in energy that only comes with *him*. My pulse stumbles, then sprints.

He steps up beside me like the bar's his stage, and he's been waiting for his cue. The faintest scent of his cologne hits me —leather, something clean and expensive —and suddenly the room feels too small, too hot. Maybe it's the coat, I might need to take this off.

I take a slow breath that doesn't help at all. My reflection in the bar mirror looks composed. My insides are anything but. He's grinning, that same glorious, infuriating smirk that should be illegal in at least half of the states. "I heard we were taking shots," he says, his voice all confidence and casual sin. "Might as well join you."

The bartender lines up the four shot glasses with the salt and a glass full of limes. I reach for mine with steady fingers that aren't actually steady at all.

I try to breathe. I fail. Because Ethan's here. And the last time he was this close, he ruined me. And from the way he's looking at me now, I know he remembers every second of it.

CHAPTER EIGHT
ETHAN

I BRING THE SHOT GLASS TO MY LIPS, BUT MY eyes never leave Olivia's.

She throws her head back like the others, the tequila making her wince, her lips parting just slightly as the heat hits her throat. She shakes her head with a soft laugh, like she's already regretting it. She has never been good at taking shots. Olivia and Tequila have never been a good combination.

God, she's trying so damn hard to play it cool, but she's not fooling anyone, at least not me. I smirk and set my glass down. Julia and Leo slide into the booth across from us. I follow Olivia in, letting her slide across the seat first, close enough that her thigh brushes against mine. It's innocently and casually. At least, that's what it would look like to anyone watching. She stiffens, just for a breath. But she doesn't move away. That's good, that's exactly what I wanted.

Across the table, Julia and Leo dive into their usual banter, the kind that turns into quick laughter and half-finished stories. It's easy for a minute. Olivia laughs at a story about Julia sneaking onto the football field after curfew, and I let myself be pulled into it, letting the rhythm of the moment settle. We start talking about work. The city, the grind, it's all surface-level, safe, way too fucking safe.

And all I can think about is the heat radiating from her skin. The way she keeps tugging her skirt down like it might cover something. I know that a mini skirt is supposed to be short, but this is way shorter than it needs to be, and she is well aware. So, I shift slightly, just enough to let my hand drift under the table, resting lightly on her thigh. She freezes mid-sentence, but she plays it cool and keeps talking. I don't move it. I just let it sit there, warm and steady.

Her eyes snap to mine, wide and filled with warning. She's about to say something, but then the server walks over, gathering empty glasses before she can talk. "Another round of shots," I say smoothly. Julia lights up. "Yes!" Olivia opens her mouth to protest, but Julia beats her to it. "Come on, O. You said you wanted to have fun tonight." Olivia exhales and gives a small smile. She looks defeated. Or maybe just tired of pretending she doesn't want this as badly as I do.

I hope for that second option. "Bring me another Bourbon with lime, please," she says casually to the server. This is getting good now.

The shots arrive. As we lift them, I let my fingers inch higher up her thigh, just an inch. Enough to make her feel me. I'm suddenly loving this mini skirt.

We knock back the shots. Olivia slams her glass down and leans in to whisper near my ear. "Stop it," she hisses, her tone is low, sharp, and completely bullshit by the smirk on her face. I lean closer, my voice just as quiet. "Why?"

Her hand grips my wrist under the table, not yanking it off, not rejecting it, just holding it. Her fingers wrap tight, like she's afraid of what happens if I go further, and fearful of what happens if I don't. She lets go, but she doesn't move away. She takes a sip of her drink, then looks at me over the rim of her glass. Her look is challenging, more like teasing. "Don't look at me like that, Liv," I murmur. She cocks her head. "Or what?" My jaw tightens. She can't be serious right now. "You really want to find out?"

Her lips twitch as if she might say yes. Like she might dare me to prove it. Across the table, Julia suddenly nudges Leo and points. "Is that Jake Henderson?"

"No way," Leo says, already standing. "We have to say hi." And they are gone. Thank you, Jake Henderson, whoever the fuck you are.

Now, it's just us. Olivia turns back to me, the tension thick between us. "Ethan, you need to—" I don't let her finish. I shift closer, my hand sliding higher onto her thigh, this time a bit faster. Her breath hitches again, but still no protest.

I lean in, my lips brushing the side of her ear. "If I

had to guess…" I pause, just long enough for her to feel it. "I'll say you're wet right now." She stiffens. Her eyes snap to mine, wide with disbelief, but she doesn't move. I press in a little closer. "Spread your legs, Liv." Her breath stutters, her jaw clenches, but she doesn't say no.

She shifts, barely, but enough. Enough for my hand to slip higher. Her skin is soft, burning hot. Every inch I move, I feel like I might lose it. The need I have for this woman is stupid, reckless, and I need to fucking stop right now. But my fingers find the edge of her panties, and I brush over the lace. I glance at her. She's biting her lip, hard. Her breath is ragged now. I slide my fingers beneath the fabric, slow and careful, until I find what I already knew would be there.

She's soaked. *Fuck*.

A low groan builds in my chest. My cock throbs hard against the zipper of my jeans. Easy, boy, we can't make a scene here. I slide one finger in, she jerks slightly, her body clenching around me. "Ethan—" she breathes. But it's not a protest, it's a prayer. Her fingers grip my wrist, but she's not stopping me. She's anchoring herself, holding on like she might fall apart if she doesn't. I curl my finger inside her, feeling her tighten, pulsing, needing me. She closes her eyes, and she sinks her teeth into her bottom lip, trying not to moan, trying not to break. I lean in again, my lips brushing her jaw, her ear, her throat. "Did you miss this?"

She doesn't answer, but she doesn't have to. The way she moves into my hand. The way her legs part a little more. The way she lets her head fall back against the booth, just slightly, that's the answer. That tells me everything I need to know.

She's *mine*.

She's *always been*.

And now? She's *finally remembering it*.

CHAPTER NINE
OLIVIA

I CLUTCH HIS WRIST, BREATH BREAKING IN shallow, uneven gasps as his finger curls inside me. This is embarrassing. He knew I was wet, but now he *knows* it. He *feels* it. Guilt hits me hard and immediately. But it doesn't stop the wave of pleasure crashing through me, doesn't stop my hips from tilting into his touch. Doesn't stop the soft, desperate whimper that slips from my lips. Fuck. I hate that I want this so badly. I hate that a part of me never stopped wanting him. "Stop," I whisper, voice wrecked. "I can't—"

Ethan's eyes drop, watching the place where his hand disappears beneath the hem of my skirt. When he looks back at me, there's something unreadable in his eyes. "You can't, what?" he murmurs.

I grit my teeth. "I—, we can't do this. Not with all these people around. Not here." What the hell did I say? Just say no, Olivia. He smirks like he expected that answer, and I want to die. It's like he knows exactly where this is going, and I have no clue. Well, I do, and it feels like I just got played in my own game. "Okay," he says, too casual for my liking. Then he slides his finger off me and laces his hand with mine. Like it belongs there, and it does. God, I missed this.

"Ethan—"

"Let's go," he says, and his voice has that edge, that low, commanding tone that makes my pulse skitter and my thighs clench. But I don't move, not an inch. "That's an order, Liv, get up." Ah fuck. Those words make me act just like a soldier responding to a command. I get up from the booth. I stand on shaky legs, letting him lead me through the bar, past the murmuring crowd, past the Out of Order sign on the restroom door, to a shadowed hallway at the back.

He pushes open a door I recognize, the manager's office, where we used to sneak in and make out all the time. He steps inside, holding the door for me. I hesitate. I feel my pulse pounding in my throat. "You can't be serious." His eyes darken, and I can see it. He is serious. "I'm dead serious." Yeah, I knew it. I step inside, and the door clicks shut behind me. He locks it, and the silence wraps around us.

He takes a step closer. Oh, I'm so fucked. "Take off your panties." My breath catches, my skin is hot. I'm sure I'm blushing. My fingers twitch at my sides, but they move. Before I can second-guess myself, I hook my thumbs under the lace and slide them down, slowly, like I'm putting up a show just for him. Maybe I am. My heart races as I step out of them. Ethan bends, picks them up off the floor, and smirks as he tucks them into his pocket like a prize he just won.

Then, he kneels. He fucking *kneels* in front of me. His voice is strong, but soft in a way that makes my knees weak. "Pull your skirt up and open your legs." My breath hitches, just a bit. "Now." The word drops like a match in gasoline. I lift my skirt with trembling hands, slowly parting my thighs. His hands find them instantly, thumbs dragging across my skin as his lips press into the inside of my knee, soft, torturous. I need his mouth on me, right about *now*. He kisses a path upward, the heat of his breath dancing over skin that hasn't been touched like this in years. "You feel so fucking good," he murmurs. And then his mouth is on me. *Finally*.

One long, slow lick. My knees nearly give out. I grip the desk behind me because it's the only thing keeping me upright. The first touch of his tongue against me sends a jolt through my spine. "Fuck," I whisper, my voice is broken. His eyes flick up. They're dark, wild, consumed.

"Liv—" he groans against me. "You taste even better than I remember." And then he devours me. His tongue moves with a skill that wasn't there sixteen years ago, but with a memory that drives me crazy. Every stroke is precise. Every flick is devastating. He licks and sucks like he has something to prove, like he's angry it's been this long. Like he's starving for me, and I don't want him to stop.

He slides one finger inside, and I gasp. Then another. The stretch is perfect. They move in sync with his tongue, slow at first, then faster, harder. My head falls back, a choked moan escaping me, "Ethan—"

"Shh," he whispers— his free hand presses to my thigh, holding me steady, grounding me as I fall apart. The pleasure builds sharply and fast. My muscles start to tremble. I can feel it coming, tight, impossible, overwhelming. "Please, I'm about to—" I whimper, fingers tangling in his hair.

But just as I'm about to come, he stops. I cry out, my hips chasing his mouth. I'm desperate for it. He stands slowly, lips still slick, fingers glistening. His eyes never leave mine. "You're not going to come, Liv," he says, voice low, thick with authority. "At least not today."

My mouth opens. "What the fuck are—" He leans in, lips brushing the shell of my ear. "You'll have to beg for it next time." My body is shaking, my thighs are wet, my heart is hammering in my chest. And even now, frustrated, denied, strung tight, I want more. Fuck, I want him. And I don't know how the hell I'm going to walk back into that bar and pretend I didn't just almost come on his mouth.

Fuck him.

CHAPTER TEN

ETHAN

SHE EXHALES, SHAKY AND WRECKED, HER HANDS trembling as they push through her hair. Her cheeks are flushed. She is still recovering from what just happened from what I just did to her. And fuck, it felt good. But then she pulls away.

"This was a mistake," she mutters, straightening her skirt, trying to smooth herself back into place. "And I won't fucking beg. Because there won't be a next time."

Her voice is sharp, final, but we both know it's a lie. "Liv," I can see it in her eyes— the panic, the heat, the way her pupils are still blown wide. "Is that so?" I ask, still tasting her on my tongue. She doesn't answer, doesn't look at me, opens the office door, and walks out like she didn't just come apart on my mouth a few minutes ago, like I didn't just feel her tremble against my hands.

I stay there, frozen, my cock still painfully hard, fists

clenched at my sides. My body is begging for her. And she just left.

Shit, I fucked this up.

I drag both hands over my face and lean against the edge of the desk, trying to steady my breathing, but her heat won't leave me. The craving won't die. And now I've got to walk back into that bar and pretend I'm not going crazy over this woman. This is a mess. What the fuck did I just do?

When I finally return to the booth, Olivia is already seated next to Julia, calm and composed. She barely spares me a glance. Her expression is unreadable, as if she had practiced before I got there. But I see the way her legs are pressed tightly together, how her nails are digging into her thigh under the table.

Leo looks up from his beer, his smirk instant. "Where'd you guys disappear to?" Olivia doesn't miss a beat. "I needed some air." Leo raises a brow but lets it slide. Julia glances at me, but if she notices anything off, she doesn't say a word. She sips her drink, eyes flicking between us like she's watching a show she already knows the ending to.

Then Olivia's phone buzzes. She glances down and freezes. Her shoulders go stiff. Her expression falters for just a second, then she slips the phone into her palm and stands without a word. If I had to guess, that was her husband calling her.

I checked mine just in case, two missed calls and a few messages from Hannah. Reality crashes in fast, cold, and merciless. I push back from the booth and follow

Olivia out into the night. The air outside is fucking freezing. She's pacing with her phone to her ear. I take a few steps in the opposite direction and call Hannah.

She picks up on the second ring. "Hey, babe."

"Hey," I say, forcing a smile into my voice. "I called earlier."

"Yeah. Sorry, I'm out with Leo and totally spaced out. We ran into some people and lost track of time." There's a pause. "Is Olivia one of those people?" My jaw clenches. "Yeah, actually, she is here with her sister, or was here, I don't see her around anymore." Liar, she is right in front of you, twenty feet away, but still *very* close to you. I don't have to lie. Hannah is not here to see it, but she knows about Olivia— not every detail, but enough.

And I know that by telling her just that, her mind will go places that it doesn't need to go. Fuck. What am I doing? She's not stupid. She knows what Olivia meant to me, means. She knows I loved her, that I haven't loved another woman the way I loved her. And that maybe I still do.

"Is she doing okay?" This woman is a saint. Even after all, she asks for her. Now I feel like a fucking piece of trash. I was just between Olvia's legs, and now I need to tell my wife that she is doing well? She was right, there won't be next time. This can't happen again. I need to apologize.

"Yeah, she seems fine." Silence stretches thin between us. Then her voice softens. "How are you holding up? I'm happy you are out. You guys deserve that," I exhale, watching Olivia pace nearby, her hand clenched into a fist. "Yeah. I'm fine. It's been good to have a little distraction." Yeah, right.

"Claire has been asking about you. Leight lost her bunny again." I huff a breath. "She's probably hiding it under the couch again." Hannah laughs, the sound familiar and warm and a little too far away. "We miss you," she says. "The girls do. I do." Guilt slices straight through me. "I miss you too." She's quiet for a moment. "Just... don't shut me out, okay?"

"I won't," I lie. "I'll let you go. Call me tomorrow?"

"Yeah. I will."

"Love you." I look over just in time to see Olivia walking my way. "Love you too." I end the call, but the tightness in my chest doesn't let up. I watch her as her shoulders sag slightly. She looks haunted. She presses a hand to her temple like the weight of everything is finally sinking in. I step forward. She holds up a hand without looking at me. "Don't."

"Liv—"

"No, Ethan, just don't." Her voice is controlled, but it's cracked at the edges. I stop, nod once, stepping back. Her phone rings again, and she answers, this time softer. "Hey. I know, I'm sorry. I got caught up." She steps away so I can't hear her conversation, but I hear just enough. "Love you too." It hits like a punch to the ribs. She ends the call, shoves her phone into her purse, and turns away from me.

"We need to talk," I say, stepping forward again. Her eyes flash. "No, we don't."

This stubborn woman. "Olivia."

"Nothing happened, Ethan. And nothing will happen again." Her voice is sharp. It feels final, like a blade cutting between us.

"We can't do this," she continues. "Not to us. Not to them." Us. Them. She's trying to draw the lines. Okay, I get it. I stare at her. My body is still humming from her taste. "You really believe that?" I ask quietly. She straightens her shoulders, lifts her chin. Looks me dead in the eye. "I have to, *we* have to." I nod slowly, biting the inside of my cheek. "Whatever you say." But we both know the truth. We've already crossed the line. And I'm not going to pretend I don't want to do it again.

CHAPTER ELEVEN
OLIVIA

THE MORNING MOVES SLOWLY, AS IF TIME ITSELF is dragging its feet, not just me. I stay in bed longer than I should, but hey, I'll take any extra sleep I can. I need it. My body is exhausted, and it looks like my mind is competing with it. I can barely keep my eyes open right now. Last night is still lingering in my head. His hands, his mouth, the way he said my name, like it still belonged to him.

I sigh and grab my phone. Two messages. Not from David, not from work. From him.

> Ethan: Sorry about last night, you were right. We crossed a line, well, I crossed a line, and we shouldn't have. This isn't fair to you, to me, or to them.

> Ethan: I let myself go. I got caught in the moment. It can't happen again. It shouldn't. We shouldn't... fuck

Ethan: Coffee as a peace offering?
Joe's 10:00 a.m.?

I look at the time, it is 9:27 a.m. I don't know what the hell to reply. What can I say? I'm aware of what happened, and while he is blaming himself, I can only think that I'm equally guilty. Yes, we did cross a line, and no, we shouldn't be doing that. But this isn't entirely his fault. I didn't stop him. And if I'm being honest with myself, I don't know if I'll stop him if he tries something again.

BY THE TIME I pull into Joe's parking lot, it's 9:53 a.m. And of course, he is already there. I'm never late to anything, but today, I didn't want to be the first one here. He is on the same table we used to sit back in the day. The one that has "the best" view. It just looks out onto the street, but it is the only window where you can see the old church and the mountains in the background, so it does offer a nice view. Being here, it feels like no time has passed. Like we are still those kids who once fell in love.

And while I hate to admit it, the memory feels nice.

I sit on the seat in front of him, my heart is pounding, and I can't even look him in the eye. Why am I so nervous? He is the one who wanted to talk. We are adults, we can have a nice conversation. We just need to admit we were wrong, apologize, and promise never to do it again. Right?

He starts to speak, but I lift a finger to shush him. The first sip of coffee is sacred, and I haven't had one yet, so he needs to wait. After that first sip warms my body, I take a deep breath. "Okay," I say. "Friends?" This is good, this isn't too much. We don't need to talk about what we did. What for? We got this. He starts to apologize, but I cut him off.

"It was a mistake, we had a moment, alcohol was involved, there were too many memories triggered, we cave, we are aware of it. That's all."

"But," He looks so confused right now. "Ah," I stop him again, "We are adults, we can move on without having to talk about it." He tilts his head, trying to understand why I am being so calm. And truth is, I would kill to know too. "Just like that?"

"Yep, just like that." I extend my hand to shake his. We do, and then we actually move on.

Or so I thought, because then he messes it up. "I always thought about calling you again." If he thought about it, why didn't he then? "But I wasn't sure if you wanted to hear from me after the way we ended things." Oh, I see. "Well, I felt horrible, thanks for asking sixteen years later." We laugh, which at this point isn't uncommon in our conversations. I don't know if we laugh because this is strange, awkward even, or if maybe it's just the pain trying to play cool. Then his voice drops. "When I left, I thought I was doing you a favor."

"How did you think dumping your girlfriend, who you planned your entire life with, over the phone, was a favor?" I'm honestly baffled.

"Not that", he looks nervous, and I'm enjoying this now. I got over the fact that he dumped me over the phone. I moved on from that. But I never moved on from *him*. "I wasn't in the right state of mind, Liv. I didn't have my life figured out like I told everyone."

"Ethan, you were 19 years old. Of course, you didn't have your life figured out. That was the point of leaving this place." Now, I can see it. He felt lost and didn't want to drag me with him. "I'm not trying to complicate things or anything, and I know we said we'll be friends moving forward, but I just... I need you to know that Tacoon wasn't home, California wasn't home. It was you. It's always been you."

"Ethan—" I grip my mug a little tighter. He needs to stop. We can't go back to this rabbit hole. Not again. We already did this when he moved out of Tacoon for college, we did it again when I started planning to move away after high school, and then again when he dumped me. "I just wanted to tell you, that's all."

I nod, and then I don't know what happened, I just spilled the worst, most truthful thought. "I moved to the city to forget you." Fuck Olivia, why can't you just shut up? He tilts his head, but his eyes don't drop mine. "Did it work?"

"What do you think?" He laughs, I laugh, we treat it as a joke, and honestly, it was for the best. After that, the conversation just kept coming like time hadn't passed.

We start talking about our kids, work, and our cities. We talk about everything except about him and her. And that's okay by me.

I don't need to talk about his perfect wife, and there's nothing about David that he needs to know. What shocked me most was that we talked about everything, just like when we were best friends. And that sucks, because he isn't that person to me anymore.

We said our goodbyes and carried on with our days.

This was nice, really. We needed this. We needed to talk without any complications, to act like we were friends again. But that's all this was, an act.

We'll never be friends again. As much as we try to convince ourselves of it, we can't. There's so much history between us, so much love, so much loss. But, we sure can pretend.

CHAPTER TWELVE
ETHAN

MY PHONE BUZZES IN MY POCKET. I ANSWER before the second ring. "Ethan, we've got a problem. The contractor just backed out of the city project. If we don't lock someone else in now, the whole thing goes to hell."

I blow out a breath and drag a hand through my hair. This can't be fucking happening. "You serious?" This is the first project we have in the city. There's no way this will go to hell. "Dead serious. We need you here. Now." Fuck my life. "Got it. I'll settle some things here and head out." I hang up, already moving around the guest house. I spot Leo at the doorstep, but I don't have time for this. "Hey man, I was going to ask you if you wanted to hit the downtown later today with Dad and Maggie."

"I would love that, but work called. There's a problem in the city with a new project, and I need to get there ASAP. "Oof, that bad?" I exhale harder than I intended to. "Yeah, that bad," and as soon as I say so, I can see Leo's brain working overtime to compute what he is about to say. This dude is going to be the death of me. Funny of me joking about death during this time, but mom wouldn't want us to be all sad forever.

"I'll go with you." I love that he means well, but he'll be bored as hell there. "It's a six-hour drive, so we'll need to stay overnight. Maybe even two nights, depending on how bad things are over there." He nods. "Sounds like a road trip. But I want my own bedroom," I roll my eyes and start packing. I'm halfway through zipping my duffel when my phone lights up again. I'll be dammed if this is another work emergency. What else could go wrong now?

Olivia: Hey, can we talk? Call me.

I don't even think twice, I'm already calling her. I should've taken my time, but she picks up immediately. "Ethan, you didn't have to call me so quickly. I could've waited." I know, I shouldn't have. "I had the phone in my hand." I can hear her laughing on the other side. "What happened?"

"So, remember the box and the letter, umm, Larna left me?" How could I forget? "Yeah, of course, what happened?" I don't know if I can take another of my mother's surprises. "Well, the box was kinda locked. The lawyer called because he found the key and wanted to give it to me. Where are you? Are you busy? I feel like we should talk about this in person."

"I'm actually packing, I leave for the city in about half an hour." There's silence in the other line. "Can I come with?" She wants to go with me. To the city? Why? "I need to be there the whole day tomorrow, so I will probably spend the night there. We can talk tomorrow when I'm back. If that works for you." She stays quiet for a minute and then... "That's okay, I'll go with you, I'll stay home and come back with you tomorrow whenever you finish your things. I need to go by the office anyway, and I could go and see the boys and David."

Yeah, sure, I'll take her with me to the city so she can see her husband. "In that case, I'll be out the door in 20 minutes." Why the hell did I say that? "Sounds good, I'll pack really quickly and be ready when you come."

Leo's smile fades. I guess he was really looking forward to a road trip. But nope, that's not it. As soon as I hang up, all I hear is... "You do remember you're married, right?" How can I forget? "Uhm, yes. I do remember. But thank you for the reminder." What is his problem? "I'm just saying," He shrugs his shoulders and gives me a 'you are about to fuck this up' kind of look.

"And what exactly are you saying?" I shouldn't get into a fight with him right now, but I can't take this. No one knows about what happened between us, and I intend to keep it that way. Not even my brother can know.

"I'm saying be careful. I know you guys are friends, if that's what you call your ex. But you are married, she's married, you guys just saw each other for the first time in a while, and you're grieving, emotions can be all over the place, and I— just be careful, man." Damn it. I can't even be mad at him. He is right about everything. But this isn't the grief talking. What I'm feeling about her is much more than what's happening right now. I know the timing isn't ideal, and maybe from the outside it can look that way, but God help me, it is not.

I'M outside her house waiting for her. Just like I used to do back in the day. The memories hit hard and fast. I can still picture the last time I was here. It was over Christmas break in my first year of college. I was about to go back to California, and neither of us knew that was our last Christmas together. Or even our last night together. We have spent most of the night at my parents' guest house. That was the last time I touched her, the last time I made her *mine*.

She opens the door, and while I thank her for the interruption down memory lane, I suddenly forget how to breathe. Black leggings, sports bra, oversized coat. Hair in a messy bun. I don't know what the hell is happening right now. I just know I'm fucked.

"You're staring," she says, sliding into the passenger seat. "Sorry. Couldn't help it." She laughs it up. "You ready?" No, the hell I'm not. "Are you?" Is she ready to spend the rest of the day with me in a car? She throws her arms up. "Woohoo. Road trip with my friend. Hell yeah, I'm ready." She's not.

I laugh as I start the engine, and off we go.

THE FIRST FEW hours are easy. Windows are cracked, the music is at a perfect volume where we can talk, be silent, or sing along. She asks about the contractor, about the whole project blowing up. She listens like she used to — like she actually cares. Maybe she still does.

It slowly started raining, then it poured. By the way traffic is looking right now, I know the drive will take easily one more hour than it's supposed to. "Looks like we're stuck here for a bit," she says. "Yep," I tap the steering wheel. "Twenty questions?" I know it's a stupid idea, but it's the only one I have right now. She hums. "Sure." The game starts light. We discuss coffee orders and the last concert we went to. First grown-up job after we left town.

Then I go a bit deeper, "What did you like most about me?" I think I know the answer to this, but I had to ask her. She smirks but doesn't hesitate to answer. "Your eyes. And the way you used to look at me. Like I was everything to you." I swallow hard. She *was* everything to me for more time than I care to admit.

"My turn." She says with a dangerous smirk on her face, one that tells me that she's not going to play nice anymore. "What's the dirtiest thought you've had about me...lately?" Shit, I was right. But I can't answer that— at least not with the truth. "And be honest." Oh fuck.

"It was just now. That you take off your leggings, recline that seat back, and I watch as you touch yourself until you're soaked. Until I feel the need to touch you and taste you. Right here, in this truck." Her breath stutters. I can see it. She shifts in her seat without saying a word. She starts reclining the seat and pulls her leggings down, just an inch, to tease me. Then she laughs, pulls her leggings back up, and adjusts the seat. "You wish, Ethan Cole. You wish." I shake my head. She almost gave me a heart attack right here.

"You are something else, Olivia." She laughs, for real this time, and that's refreshing. But then all of a sudden, her expression changes.

CHAPTER THIRTEEN
OLIVIA

I STARE AT HIM, "SO, I REALLY DON'T KNOW HOW to say this, but I opened your mom's box and read the letter." Oh God, this will be harder than I thought. I should've waited for him to open it. Right? It was his mom. It is his mom. Ugh! "Okay, so what's in the box and what did the letter say?" Ah, I don't want to tell him, I can't do this.

Olivia, suck it up. You decided to put yourself in this position. Now be a grown woman.

"Okay, you need to pick one. The box or the letter, and then on our way back, we'll talk about the other thing. Deal?" Yes, this is better. This way, I don't have to deal with both at once. Now, I hope he picks the letter. He is looking at me like I just rigged the game, and honestly, I love this feeling. "Let's do the letter. But you don't need to read the whole thing. It was meant for you, and I appreciate you wanting to share it with me, but it's yours."

I hate this side of him, so noble, so sweet. No, focus. "Okay, that's fair, I'll read you some parts that I know you might want to hear." He nods, turning the music down. I take the letter out of my bag, and I can sense his eyes on me as I take it out of the envelope.

'My sweet girl, if you are reading this, it means I'm not here anymore, which sucks, I know.'

We both laugh. This is so her.

'I always wanted you to have this, and I know that under different circumstances you would've.'

I feel his eyes penetrating my skin. I know he understands what this is about, and now I'm scared. It's raining, so he's pretending to be focusing on the road rather than on me, but that's bullshit.

'I loved you like a daughter, you were and always will be part of our family, no matter where life takes you. This meant a lot to me, and I know it meant a lot for Ethan too.'

I stop right there, I don't want to keep reading, and I know I don't need to. He understood. The rain slams against the windshield like it's in a bad mood, and we are stopping in the middle of the road. "Let's table this conversation for now." He says to roll the window down as an officer approaches the truck. "Hey, officer, what's going on?"

"There's a bad accident on the bridge, we had to close it, and we got a tornado watch just now, so we're pulling everyone off the road." Ah, great, just what we needed, more time alone together to finish the conversation I don't want to have. He nods, rolling the window up, and glances at me. "Should we look for a hotel or something?"

He had to be joking. "A hotel in the middle of nowhere? You are really confident, sir. But what we're going to find here is a run-down motel at its best." He looks at me like I'm stupid. "You have a better idea? Because we could drive back, but we are four hours in already, and still, we'll need to wait out the tornado."

I hate this so much, and I can't believe I'm about to say this, but hell. "Okay, let me see what I can find. Take this exit on the right, and we can stop nearby if needed." And as soon as I say that and he takes the exit, it's like God or the Devil heard me. Because down the road, in flashing neon lights, it says 'MOTEL'. I look at him and put my hand out. "Voila, there you go. I found a motel." He laughs and drives to it.

THIS HAS to be the worst place I have ever been. The rug sounds as you walk on it. I don't mean you can hear the floor underneath, I'm saying you can actually hear the carpet. Which means that it has been wet more times than it has been dry. That's scary. And unsanitary for sure. We approach the counter, and I can see the keys in those little boxes in the back of the wall. I feel like I'm in a movie, but not the good kind, more like a scary type of shit where you know someone is going to die from the beginning. I don't know if I'm saying this in my mind or out loud, but Ethan is looking at me like I'm insane. "You need to stop."

"Stop what?" Oh shit, I must have said something out loud. "You are spiraling. It looks like you are in a scary movie and are finding a way not to die, but you are dying anyway." Yep, he is in my head, which is worse than saying something out loud. "Okay, you need to get out of my head. And this looks exactly like that." He rolls his eyes at me and approaches the lady at the counter.

"Can we have two rooms, please, just for one night?" She looks between us and checks the wall for the keys, but as she is about to grab them, a guy in the next computer grabs one of the keys. I search for another one, but I don't see any. "Oh, sorry, it looks like we only have one room left." Ethan inhales and exhales louder than necessary. "That's okay. Is it a double bedroom?"

She checks the computer, "No, sorry, it's a single room." He looks at me, and I look at him. We're not saying anything. We don't have to. "Okay," he says as he takes the key. "I'll sleep on the floor," he whispers to me. And we are off to the room.

When he opens the door, I look at him, look at the rug, look at him again. "You are not sleeping on this floor." This rug is as dirty as the road outside. Okay, I'm exaggerating, but he can't sleep there. He laughs and nods. Well, this should be interesting. I drop my bag, peel off my wet jacket, and redo my hair in a bun.

"Can I call dibs on the shower?" I nod, prepping the bed for what is going to be the worst sleepover in history. Two exes trapped in a motel, after they almost have sex in an office in a bar downtown, who are pretending to be just friends because they are both married. Yeah, sounds about right.

I sit on the edge of the bed, watching him get ready for his shower, and I can't help but wonder what he looks like naked now. It's been a long time since I saw him, and he saw all of me the other day, which isn't fair. I'm tired of pretending I didn't enjoy it. And more so, I'm tired of pretending I regret it. I look up, and he's already watching me.

"What's on your mind, Liv?" The answer is simple. "You."

He looks at me like he was waiting for that answer. "I'm right here." And that's the problem, he is right *here*, in front of me, in a motel room. I could be a responsible adult and ignore it, take a shower, go to bed, and be on our way in the morning. But with him, I'm not that. I'm not capable of being that. "We should fight this," I say.

"We should," he agrees, stepping toward me. "Then why are you walking towards me?" And just like that, the tension's back. That same feeling we had at the attorney's office, the same thing at the bar. This heat I can't control when I'm around him. This feeling makes me want to forget about everything and risk it all. His hand brushes a piece of hair from my face. "Say no," he murmurs. "I'll stop."

I don't say anything because what could I say? Instead, I stand up and kiss him. The first kiss is slow, just like the first we ever had. And I have to say, I was the one who kissed him that first time. I don't think he remembers that, but I do. Then the kiss escalates. There's nothing sweet or soft about what's going on here. His mouth moves like it owns mine, and right now, it does.

I drag him closer, pull at his shirt, and we tumble into the bed. He strips me down in seconds, leggings, panties, bra, all gone. His mouth leaves trails down my neck, over my chest, everywhere. When I tug at his belt, he groans. It's low, but I hear him, jeans hitting the floor fast. I can feel him pressing against me. He's not wearing anything under those jeans. Heaven can't help me now. And that's when his fingers slide between my legs.

"Fuck," he breathes. "You're soaked." I meet his eyes. "That's your fault." He kisses me again, then presses against me, teasing me. "Tell me no, I'll stop Olivia." I could, and I should. I shake my head, but I say yes, and kiss him again. That's all he needed.

We don't speak or ask anything, but I see him trying to reach for his bag, and I feel like I should say it. "I have an IUD, we don't need to—" he nods, "That's okay, then we—," I interrupt him, "Yeah, okay, perfect, let's—" He didn't let me finish, he just kissed me again.

He pushes into me, and I gasp. The stretch, the fullness, everything is like I remember it, but bigger and better. I moan into his lips, and he kisses me deeper. His thrusts start slow, deep like he's savoring it. Like he's reclaiming something. His hands grip my hips, and my nails dig into his back. I lift my hips to meet him, and when I feel him that deep, a moan escapes me, and he groans. "I used to dream about this. About you moaning my name." My brain short-circuits, and when I think I could speak, his fingers find my clit, and that's it for me.

"Ethan, don't stop—" He smirks. "Are you begging?" I roll my eyes, he laughs, and thrusts deeper. "I won't stop, not until you're done." I fall apart. It slams into me hard, and my whole body is shaking. My thighs are trembling. I cry out, muffled against his shoulder as the orgasm rips through me.

He follows, hips stuttering. "Liv, I'm...fuck—"

"Don't stop," I gasp. I want to feel him finish inside of me. I missed this, and if we're doing it, I need to feel it all. His groan is raw as he spills into me, his body pressed tight to mine. Then, slowly, he slides out, only to push back in again, slow and deep, making me gasp. And then he holds me like he's afraid I'll vanish. And I cling to him like I just might.

We stayed like that for a while, his arms around me, my cheek pressed against the familiar shape of his chest. The storm outside is a living thing, rattling the windows, throwing flashes of light across the room. But in here, it's still. Quiet. Like the rest of the world, it finally gave us permission to stop pretending.

The clock ticks somewhere behind us. The air smells like rain and dust and *him*. "I should hate you," I say into the silence, my voice small, half swallowed by the thunder. "For making me feel like this again." His breath catches before he answers. "I should hate myself," he says, voice low and uneven.

I turn in his arms. He doesn't flinch. His eyes find mine, tired, tender, full of something that feels like grief and hope tangled together. "I loved you so much," I whisper. He nods, swallowing hard. "I never stopped." That does it. The tears come, hot and fast. I hate that I'm crying. I hate crying, but these aren't tears of regret. This doesn't feel like a mistake. It feels inevitable. Like gravity, like coming home. They're for the years we lost. For every word we swallowed, every phone call we didn't make. For every night, I tried to convince myself I was fine.

"I built a life trying to forget you," I say quietly. My throat feels tight. "Every decision I made after you, it was like I was trying to build proof that I'd moved on." He shakes his head. "I built my life trying to deserve you." That shatters something in me I didn't know was still fragile.

For a long moment, neither of us moves. Then I reach for his hand, slow, uncertain, like it's the first time all over again. He laces his fingers through mine and holds tight. It's not desperate, it's just steady.

We don't say anything else. There's nothing left to explain.

The storm keeps raging, rain thrashing the glass, wind howling like it's mourning something too. And still, we stay there, wrapped in silence and in each other, letting the world outside fall apart.

CHAPTER FOURTEEN
ETHAN

THE MORNING SUN COMES UP SLOWLY, LIKE IT'S not sure it should be here yet. The rain stopped. The storm's gone. At least the one outside is. Because whatever happened last night was its own kind of disaster— a beautiful, impossible, completely wrong mess. And yeah, I should probably hate myself for it. I should be full of guilt. My brain should wrap around all the logic and reasons why this can't happen again.

But I'm not. Not even close.

She's lying on her side, one leg kicked out from under the blanket, the sheet twisted around her waist. Hair everywhere. Her face is half-buried in the pillow. Completely wrecked and beautiful. For a minute, I just stand there, watching her breathe. That soft rise and fall that makes my chest feel tight. She looks peaceful, and I know it's temporary. Any second now, she'll wake up, and reality will crash back in. I scrub a hand over my face, sigh, and look around. I need coffee.

The motel machine is a relic, the kind that gurgles and wheezes like it's dying, spitting out something that technically qualifies as caffeine. I fill it up with tap water, drop in one of those sad little packets, and hit "brew." It starts dripping, slow and uneven. I lean against the counter, watching the steam rise, trying not to think. But of course, I think about last night. About how she looked at me like she wanted to hate me and couldn't. About how I told myself to stop, but didn't

The smell of coffee must've woken her. I hear the sheets rustle behind me, but I keep my eyes on the sink, pretending I didn't notice. The air feels heavier with her awake.

I step into the bathroom and turn on the shower. The pipes groan for a second before the water evens out. Steam starts to fill the small space, curling up the mirror until my reflection disappears. For a few seconds, the sound of the water is the only thing that makes sense. Then there's a knock— soft, a bit hesitant. "Can I come in?" Part of me wants to say no, because that would be the smart move. But of course, she can come in. I tried to play it cool earlier, but I'm dying to kiss her again, to touch her. I smile. "You're already halfway there."

The door creaks open. She steps inside, barefoot, one hand rubbing at her face, hair a wild mess of sleep. "Just need to wash my face and mouth," she mutters. The shower's already running. The water drums against my shoulders and the tile. I nod toward the sink. "It's all yours."

She's looking at me, and I'm letting her. She leans

over the basin, splashes her face, and glances up, catching my reflection in the fogged mirror. "Room for one more?" I tilt my head, grinning. "Get in here." Her breasts bounce as she lifts the hoodie over her head. My cock twitches immediately. She's not wearing panties, and I don't know what to look at, so I settle for her eyes.

She gets in, ignoring me and going straight to the water. I stand behind her, and as soon as I kiss her neck, she twists and meets my lips. And while I'm craving her kisses, I'm dying to be between her legs again.

I drop to my knees, and I pull one of her legs over my shoulder and spread her open. Eyes on hers the whole time. I want her squirming. As soon as my tongue touches her, she rocks into my mouth. I slide one finger into her and curl it up. She nearly collapses. "Ethan, fuck —" This is precisely how I want her. I stand up, lift her fast, her legs around my waist. My cock presses against her, hard and ready. She's soaked. I slide into her slowly and deep, and we both groan. She clenches around me instantly.

This time is rough. Neither of us is stopping to even think about the next move. Every thrust tighter than the last. Her nails dig into my back, her mouth finds my neck, her breath is ragged. She comes hard, head back, eyes shut, my name on a gasp. I don't last long after that. I bury myself deep and groan her name, hips stuttering as I let go inside her.

We stand there for a while, pressed together under the water, breathing each other in.

We finish our shower, dry off, and get out. She's

about to walk back to the bed to get dressed when I stop her with a hand on her wrist. "Drop the towel." She freezes. "Lie down," I say, voice low. "And spread your legs."

She nods, drops the towel, and sits on the bed with her legs wide open.

Now, this is a view.

CHAPTER FIFTEEN
OLIVIA

His voice alone makes my stomach clench and makes me wet.

I should be embarrassed of thinking like that, but at this point, I don't even care anymore. So, I lose the towel, sit on the bed, and open my legs. He drops his towel and fuck me. He looks good. Last night I couldn't see it all, and in the shower, everything happened so fast that I didn't have time to admire his body.

He is all muscle, he is *big*, and he's staring at me right now. He kneels between my thighs and spreads me open. His eyes lock on mine, then his mouth is on me. The first lick wrecks me. My hips jerk, a moan escapes, loud and needy. I grab at the sheets. My breath is ragged, my thighs are already shaking. His tongue moves slowly, then faster. Teasing me, torturing me. Like he knows exactly what I need and exactly how to hold back until I break.

A finger slides in. I arch off the bed with a moan. His other hand finds my breast, thumb circling my nipple until it's tight and aching. He looks up at me, eyes dark, focused. Watching me fall apart. "You about to finish?" he asks, voice low. I nod, wild and breathless. "Good," he says. "Do it in my mouth." And I do. My whole body clenches, legs shaking, toes curling, fingers digging into the sheets. But he doesn't stop.

And that's when I feel something I have never felt before. A rush came through me. I felt like I was going to explode. He kept going, two fingers in, curled up, his mouth on me, licking through it, drawing it out until I'm gasping for air. His other hand pressed lower in my stomach until I lost all the control I had left. This has never happened before. "Good girl." He says as he kisses my thigh like it's a reward.

I'm all over his face, his hands, the sheets. I'm still shaking and trying to remember how to breathe. I bury my face in my arm, half-embarrassed, half-high. He crawls up and kisses me. I can taste myself on his tongue. Then he pulls back and grins. "Was that your first time squirting?" I nod. My cheeks are on fire. I'm not embarrassed about sex. I love sex, but I hate being surprised or feeling out of control, and *this* was both.

He starts walking backward to the chair across the room where he put his towel earlier. "I'm honored to be your first. *Again*." I smile at him as I mutter "Fuck you," Because fuck him, but also *fuck him*.

He sits down and starts stroking himself, and I'm here salivating for this man. "Come here," and as I stand, he puts his other hand up, "uh uh, crawl," he says, signaling the floor. And God help me, but I got on my knees with no hesitation, and I hated this rug. When I reach him, he grabs my face with one hand and, with the other, guides himself into my mouth. I watch his eyes close as I stroke with one hand, and I take him deep, tongue swirling, lips tight. His groan is low and rough, his hips twitching. His hands slide into my hair, guiding me. "Fuck, Liv. I'm close."

I keep going, faster, deeper. "I want to finish in your mouth," he says. "If you want that, of course." I meet his eyes. Nod once and keep going. He groans, spilling into my mouth. I swallow all of it, I don't even flinch. And I don't look away. He pulls me up and kisses me hard. He didn't even care he just finished in my mouth. And fuck that's even hotter.

Then, without a word, he grabs me, pushes me into the bed, spreads my legs, and slides into me in one deep thrust. I gasp. My nails digging into his shoulders, I moan, he moans, it's a mess. He moves like he already memorized every inch of my body, and I let him. Every stroke hits deeper. I wrap my legs around him, hands in his hair, breath stuttering. "Ethan—" I choke out.

His eyes are locked on mine. "I can't get enough of you, Olivia. I can't stop." And I don't want him to. He pulls me on top as he sits on the bed. I ride him slowly, grinding into him until his hands find my breasts, teasing my nipples, making me cry out again. We finish together this time, moaning into each other's mouths, our bodies shaking. And if I had to choose, this is my new favorite sex memory of us.

After our first time, of course. "Was it always like

that?" His voice pulls me out of the fog I've been drifting in.

"What?"

"Us," he murmurs. "The way we... fit. Was it always like that, or did I forget?" I turn my head toward him. The ceiling is pale gray in the early light, the kind of light that makes everything look more honest than you want it to. His hand is warm against mine, fingers brushing the edge of my palm like he's afraid I'll pull away.

"You clearly didn't forget," I say, and a laugh slips out before I can stop it, soft, uneven, a nervous laugh more than anything. He exhales, eyes still on the ceiling. "Tell me this isn't just nostalgia or grief," he says quietly. "Tell me I'm not the only one who feels like you still belong to me."

I should lie. God, I should. I should give him the practical answer, the responsible one. The one that lets us both off the hook. But my throat tightens around the truth. "You're not the only one." We fall into silence.

For a while, we just stare at the ceiling, the weight of everything pressing down on us. I can almost feel the next thought rising in him, the one that will pull us backward again, and I need to stop it. I need to move this to a safer place before I drown in it.

"Can we go back to the conversation we were having on our way here yesterday?" He says his voice is low.

"That's all I wanted to read about the letter, at least for now, and we agreed we won't discuss the box until we go back." He nods. "Also, I guess by now you should imagine what's in the box." He nods again. He doesn't say anything, and neither do I.

The reality is that the letter and the box would've changed everything sixteen years ago, hell, even ten years ago. But now? Now we can't. It's not our time, and despite the bubble we are in right now, we both know this can't happen ever again.

"I need to say something. You're not going to like it, I don't even like it, but someone has to say it." He sits down on the bed and murmurs, "I know what you are going to say, and you're right." Does he really? I feel like we are still in the post sex haze. "We can't do this again. We had our little adventure here, our bubble, but as soon as we walk out of that door, this needs to remain here."

He nods, looks at me, and says, "You are mine, Olivia, always have been, always will be," kissing my thigh.

This man is the death of me.

And then the wake-up call arrives. Pun absolutely intended. His phone buzzes on the nightstand, cutting through the quiet like it's been waiting for the perfect moment to ruin everything. He glances at the screen, then at me. A split second of hesitation, before he picks it up and walks into the bathroom.

The door clicks shut, but the walls in this place are paper-thin. I don't even have to lean in to hear him. And now, I feel like shit. 'Yeah, love you too.' Nope, I was wrong, *now* I feel like actual shit.

What was I thinking? He has a wife. I have a husband. And yet here I am, wrapped in the mess we made. I sit up, pull the blanket around me like that'll help, elbows on my knees, head in my hands.

What kind of woman does this? Why did I let it happen? The questions come fast, tripping over each other, and I can't answer a single one. Then, just as quickly, the truth hits, ugly and simple and undeniable.

I'm the kind of woman who's still in love with her first love.

I'm doing this because I love *him*. Because somewhere between growing up, getting married, and pretending to move on, I never really stopped.

'I'm doing this because I love him. I never stopped loving him.' I repeat to myself as I groan and drag a hand down my face. "Oh, fuck me," I whisper into the empty room.

CHAPTER SIXTEEN
ETHAN

SHE'S ALREADY DRESSED WHEN I STEP OUT OF the bathroom. She has her hair pulled back, shoes on, and a bag in her hand like she's been ready for hours. Her eyes slide past me, not unfriendly, just... guarded.

I don't know how to face her after that call. I know this isn't easy. I know it looks worse than it sounds and feels worse than either of us will admit. I also know exactly what's tearing me apart. I just told my wife I love you. The words came out on instinct, years of habit, muscle memory. And now, standing here, looking at Olivia, I want to say it again, this time to her.

I love them both. How the hell does that even happen?

I thought I buried her a long time ago. I told myself she was a chapter that ended. But the truth is, I never closed that book. I just threw a blanket over it and pretended it wasn't there. And yes, I always knew I loved her, past tense, safe tense. But standing here, watching her zip her jacket and avoid my eyes, I know it's still *now*.

She's not just someone I loved. She's the one I can't stop loving.

I'm so completely and hopelessly fucked.

"Are you ready?" I ask because it's the only sentence I can manage. She nods, eyes on the door. "Yeah." Great. So that's where we are now. Her being quiet, me pretending silence counts as control.

We walk out together, neither of us says another word.

THE STORM'S GONE. The roads are clear, and everything outside looks calm again. She's in the passenger seat, scrolling through her phone like she's already somewhere else, back in her other life, the safe one.

My hands tighten around the wheel until my knuckles ache. The silence between us is brutal. Too many words sitting in it, unsaid. She's shutting down. Same as always. And I'm supposed to sit here and let her?

"Hey, Liv—"

"Don't." She cuts me off, voice flat, calm in a way that makes me want to shout. "It's okay. I understand." That does it. Something hot flashes through me, anger, frustration, something I don't even want to name.

"Stop doing that," I snap. "You don't even know what I was going to say."

"I have a feeling," she mutters, still staring at her screen. "Let's just leave it." No. Not this time. I yank the truck over onto the shoulder, tires kicking up gravel, the engine growling under the strain. She lurches forward, wide-eyed. "Ethan! What the hell?" I throw it in park, jaw locked, heart hammering so hard it hurts.

The world outside is blindingly bright, sunlight flashing off puddles, the air sharp and cold through the half-open window. Inside the cab, everything feels too small, too close. I unbuckle my seat belt and turn toward her. She looks at me like she's trying to decide whether to be angry or afraid.

"I can't keep pretending this doesn't matter," I say, the words rough, unsteady. "You can shut down all you want, but I'm still here, and this—*whatever this is*—it's not nothing."

She exhales, shaky. For a second, neither of us moves. Her eyes meet mine, full of everything we shouldn't say. She stiffens, then breaks. Her hands grip my hair. She kisses me like she needs to. Like it's the only thing that makes sense. Because right now it is. When we finally stop, I press my forehead to hers, breathing hard. "I can't do this halfway. I'm not built like that. I love you, Liv. I've always fucking loved you." There it is, I said it, and for some reason, I don't feel lighter or better.

She doesn't pull away, doesn't say anything. Instead, she climbs onto my lap. Straddles me right there in the driver's seat. "I love you too," she looks wrecked, but this feels so honest. "I don't know what this is. But I love you."

That's it. I'm done. No going back now.

She kisses me again, hard as she starts undoing my belt and freeing me. I pull up her dress and move her panties to the side. "Liv," I groan. I'm already losing control. She sinks onto me, slowly, and I'm deep inside of her. She rides me slowly, doing filthy rolls with her hips. I thrust up to meet her, matching her rhythm. I push her forward, bracing her on the steering wheel, fucking her harder, deeper. Her nails clawing into the seat, her body tightens as she comes. Her legs are shaking, she's panting. A few more thrusts and I'm groaning, spilling into her, hips jerking.

Neither of us says a word, not for the rest of the ride.

All I can think right now is that she didn't say anything when I said I couldn't do this halfway. She did say 'I love you' and that should be enough, but being realistic, what could I expect from her? That she leaves her husband and comes to live with me, and we all become a great big, beautiful family? That's ridiculous. What am I even thinking right now? There's no way in hell I could go to Hannah and say, 'Hey, I still love Olivia, could we talk about this and what this might entail?'

You are such an idiot, Ethan.

By the time we reach the site, the sky's a washed-out blue, and the sun's back, pretending nothing happened. The road dust sticks to the windshield, and the smell of wet pavement still hangs in the air.

"Give me three, maybe four hours," I tell her. My voice comes out rough, like I've been punched in the throat. And I have been, just not by her, by myself.

She nods once, eyes straight ahead. "Okay." That single word lands heavier than it should. We roll to a stop beside the fence line. The truck idles loudly in the quiet. I can see the site up ahead, the half-finished framing, piles of lumber, plastic tarps flapping in the wind. A perfect mess, just waiting for someone to make sense of it. Kind of like us. I open my mouth, trying to find something, anything, that might patch the silence. "Liv, I—"

"I know." Her voice is barely there, a whisper that could mean a thousand things. She doesn't look at me. Just stares out the windshield. "Just go." I stare at her for a second longer, wishing she'd look back, give me something, a sign, a word, anything to hold onto. But she doesn't. So, I grab my bag and step out into the wind. The door shuts harder than I mean it to.

She pulls away before I've even made it to the gate. Tires crunch over gravel, taillights disappearing down the road without a single glance in the mirror. I stand there for a long minute, thinking about everything I should've said but didn't.

CHAPTER SEVENTEEN
OLIVIA

I PULL INTO THE DRIVEWAY AND LET OUT A LONG breath when I see the lights on. Beatriz's car is parked out front, and no David. Thank God. I couldn't face him right now.

Inside, I'm hit with the sound of laughter from the playroom. Beatriz meets me at the door with a warm smile. "Welcome back. The kids have been asking about you all morning." I smile and set my bag down. "I missed them, too." We chat for a few minutes. She gives me the rundown— who cried, who didn't nap, what exploded in the kitchen. Beatriz keeps this place running, and I probably don't say thank you enough.

I thank her, then head upstairs to shower while texting David. 'Hey, I'm in the city for a few hours, have to stop by the office to work on a crisis, want to grab lunch?' That's a half lie, because it's true, that's happening, just not to me.

I hate lying. I don't even know when I became so good at it.

The moment the water hits my skin, the guilt shows up. I hate this feeling, but it's all my fault. I press my palms to the wall and stand there. Because the truth is, I don't know how to fix this. I love two men.

That's the part no one warns you about when you're growing up. How sometimes love doesn't show up in neat little timelines.

One man built a life with me. The other? He's been in my bones since I was fifteen. It's a different love. But it's still love. And what just happened wasn't just nostalgia or grief, let alone closure. It cracked something wide open. And now I can't pretend I don't feel it.

I shut the water off and get out quickly. If I stay in this shower, thinking about all of this, I might kill myself. Not really, but yeah.

I get dressed, do my makeup, and head out. There's already a message from David saying yes to lunch, with a pin to a restaurant. Oh fuck, I'm on Ethan's truck. Great, now I need to park far enough away so he doesn't see me. I hate this— the lying, the secrecy, it's all too much.

David's already at the restaurant when I arrive, suited up, smiling like always. He stands when I walk in and pulls me into a hug. It's strong. Familiar. Safe. Then he kisses me. It's good. But it doesn't land the same way anymore. And I hate myself for even thinking that.

We talk about everything. About work, the kids, my mom, and what's going on at home. It's easy, it feels normal, and it's comfortable. When he says 'I love you' as we're leaving, I say it back without hesitation. Because I do love him, but now, it all feels... different.

After lunch, I've got a couple of hours before I need to pick up Ethan, so I'll go grab some coffees to go and swing by the office. It's the first time I've been here in about two weeks, and walking in feels like getting a piece of myself back.

This is great. This is just what I needed.

Monica, my assistant, lights up as soon as she sees me. "Well, well, look who finally remembered we exist," I smirk. "I brought coffee." She smiles, "Is that a bribe?"

"You know it is." We laugh it out, and she follows me to my office. "How's country life treating you?" I drop my bag and sigh. "More complicated than I planned for." She narrows her eyes. "That sounds juicy. Do we need to add vodka to our coffees?" I missed this, having her close. She is more than my assistant, and while I try to keep some boundaries, she's been a great friend over the years.

"Oh, hell no, let's stick to just coffee," She launches into a full-blown saga about her week— dumping a guy, going on a date with a girl, and lining up a third person for tomorrow. I stare at her. "You go through people faster than I go through dry shampoo."

"And yet, you love me." She grins. "Unfortunately." It's light. Easy. And for the first time in days, I don't feel like I'm suffocating. I'm catching up on some emails, since I've been avoiding my phone over the last few days. I look over some reports I need to send at the end of the week and pretend to care about a pitch meeting I've already mentally canceled. I love my job. Having my own company has been the highlight of my life, really. I never dreamt of being a mother or a wife, that just happened. But this— having something mine, something I built from the ground up— this has been my dream.

I finish up in the office and leave everything in order so everyone can survive at least one more week. I go downstairs to the coffee shop, and I grab two more coffees before I head out.

When I pull up to the site, Ethan's finishing up, tossing instructions to his crew like he's been doing this forever. He looks so confident, so in control. I love seeing this side of him. And I love this side of me with him. He spots me, smiles, and jogs over. That smile still wrecks me. I catch myself watching him longer than I should, thinking I could get used to this.

The thought hits hard. Too hard. I laugh under my breath and shake it off. He slides into the passenger seat, "What's so funny?" he asks, tossing his bag in the back.

"Nothing." I hand him his coffee. He raises an eyebrow but lets it go. "Ready to go back?" Absolutely no. I don't know if he meant to go back or to leave whatever we had behind. But I'm not ready for either.

And, as I became really good at lying, I said, "Yeah," and put the car in drive. "Let's go." As we pull onto the highway, I glance over at him. And I already know that getting out of this clean isn't going to happen.

CHAPTER EIGHTEEN
ETHAN

THE DRIVE BACK TO TACOON IS SMOOTH.

Maybe it's because we left early to beat the traffic. Or maybe it's because the roads are clear after the mess of last night. Finally, the silence between us isn't awkward. We finally said what we needed to, and I think we had enough of that.

We stopped for food at the three-hour mark, and switched so I could finish the drive. Everything has been going great. We just slipped into this old rhythm, laughing at dumb stuff, swapping stories like we're just... us again. It feels good. Too good. Which, of course, is precisely when my phone rings.

HANNAH

I shoot a glance at Olivia. She's pretending to look out the window, but I know she's paying attention. "Hey," I say, trying to keep my voice even. "Hey," Hannah replies, too calm. "Where are you?"

"Driving back. Should be home in about two hours or so." We talk about the girls— the usual stuff. Their bedtimes, snacks, work— and then her tone shifts.

"Were you with Olivia the other night?" Olivia doesn't move, but I feel her freeze. I grip the wheel tighter. "Yeah. She was there. Everybody was. We all catch up," If you can call it that. There's a pause. Long enough to be loud. "Okay, I can sense you don't want to talk about this right now," she finally says. "We'll talk when you get back."

Of course, I don't want to talk about this right now. I have her next to me, and I don't want to say anything that will hurt either of them. "Will do, love you," I say. It feels automatic, like a habit. She waits just long enough to make it hurt. "Love you too." When I hang up, Olivia doesn't say anything. Not for a beat. Then, "What was that?"

"What was what?" Me talking about her to my wife? Ah yeah, that. "Her asking about me, and you telling her you were with me." She looks at me, demanding an explanation. I sigh. "I told Hannah a long time ago I still loved you. She knew I'd see you while I was here."

"She knew?"

"Yeah. I never lied to her about that, about you. She doesn't know about... this," I gesture between us, "but she always knew about you." Olivia exhales, shaking her head. "I don't even know what to do with that information."

"I know this is complicated, and maybe unusual. Not many people will understand, and I don't feel like explaining it. I love her, and I love you. I love two women at the same time, and they both know it. Yes, it's fucked up, but it's the truth."

The thing about feeling this way is that I don't care about people understanding it. I was clear with Hannah a long time ago. She knows Olivia was the one. She was and always will be the love of my life, but the universe had other plans for us. I chose Hannah, I decided to have a life with her, and yes, maybe because I didn't have Olivia, but that doesn't mean I love Hannah any less.

"I get it," she says without hesitation. And I'm just blown away by how easily she understands me. She doesn't judge me or ask questions because she doesn't have to.

I've always been a tough guy. I don't let a lot of people get close. Olivia and Hannah are the only two women I've ever really loved.

"I don't want to end this, whatever this is between us. I know we shouldn't, but I can't, I won't do it." She doesn't say anything else, she just stares out the window for a while. "You mean a lot to me, and I already lost you sixteen years ago. I can't let that happen, not again." I can see her eyes get glassy, but she doesn't say anything.

We don't talk anymore.

WE ROLL into Tacoon around eight something. Phones buzz at the same time. Group text from Maggie: "Lulu's at 9. Be there. It's important." I groan. "It's already 8:27." Olivia reads it, lips twitching. "Quick shower, and we head out? We won't be there at 9:00 p.m., but we can make it." I nod. "I'll drop you off, head home, get ready—"

"Just shower at my house," she says, like it's nothing. "There are plenty of bathrooms, and I think my mom's not there right now, so..." I grin. "One condition." She smirks. "Let me guess... You are going to ignore the part where I said that there are enough bathrooms and will demand that I shower with you?"

"Obviously," She just laughs.

The house is empty when we get there. We head upstairs, and the second I step into her room, it's like getting slammed by a memory train. She sees it on my face and grins. "Been a while since you snuck in here."

"Yeah, back when we were reckless and horny teenagers." She laughs. "And now we are just reckless and horny adults," she says, pulling my shirt off.

I pull up her dress, take off her panties, and throw her on the bed. I don't waste time. I drop to my knees, and she opens her legs instantly, like she's been waiting for this. I put my mouth on her, and she rides my face, grabbing the sheets, moaning my name.

She's fucking perfect when she's trembling like this.

When she's done, I lift her, take her dress off, take my clothes off, and carry her into the shower, turn the water on, and press her against the wall. I fuck her like I've got something to prove. Her legs around me, the water crashing down, her moaning into my neck.

"I love you, Ethan," she gasps.

"Say that again," I growl. "I love you, Ethan," And with that, I finish. Spilling into her, holding her like I'll never let go because I won't.

Let's say we didn't arrive at Lulu's at 9:00 p.m., but we sure as hell came.

LULUS USED to be a bakery when we were in high school. Pastel bricks, sticky counters, the smell of sugar and yeast. Now it's barely recognizable, moody amber lighting, sleek black trim, and enough exposed piping to make it feel like someone airlifted what could be a Brooklyn bar into small-town Tacoon.

I can see Maggie there with Leo, and two other people I don't recognize at first.

Josh and Audrey. Fuck my life. Maggie could've warned me. We haven't had a relationship with them. I mean, we know each other, but we don't consider ourselves stepsiblings. We're more like acquaintances with the same dad, if that makes sense.

"Hey Ethan, remember Josh and Audrey?" They seem so grown up now, we all do. Josh is older than us, which makes him around thirty-nine, maybe even forty by now. Audrey, on the other hand, is younger, which is what makes this whole story messy. She has to be in the middle of Leo and me, so around twenty-six or twenty-eight.

"Hey guys, how are you?" They have that sympathy smile on their faces, like every other person at the funeral had 'I'm sorry your mom died' face. Josh is the first one to extend his hand. "Good man, I'm sorry bout Larna." I smile and nod. Audrey comes in for an unexpected hug. "I'm so sorry about your mom. She was always so nice to us." I nod again. "Yeah, she was like that." Well, this is awkward.

"Hey, I'm Olivia, a family friend." Thank God she noticed and interrupted whatever this was. "I remember you," Josh says, which tracks because they were here one Christmas when we were too young to understand all of this. "Oh yeah, Christmas at the Coles," She adds, so she remembers all this, too.

We share some more casual conversations until we get to the bottom of what we are really doing here. "So, this is the place Larna left all of us," Josh says. Maggie nods, Leo and Audrey too, and I'm just here like, what the fuck. Did the bakery belong to us this whole time? But I can't look like the idiot who didn't know anything. So, act like I know what I'm doing. And I decided to treat this as any other one of my projects.

"So, what's the plan? What did you guys have in mind?" They all seem engaged with my question. Perfect, that's what I want. "Well, we bought the two buildings next door recently, and we wanted to convert this into some bar thingy. If you guys are on board, or we wanted to buy you out if that's more appealing," Audrey says with such an attitude, but in a pleasant way that I'm surprised.

Before I can even talk, Maggie steps in, "I'll be okay with selling my share, but only to my brothers, no offense." Of course, she did that. Audrey nods, smiling, and Josh nods too.

"I can't buy you out," Leo says. Of course, he can't. He doesn't even have a savings account. "I'll buy you out, I mean, I'm not one of your brothers, but..." Olivia says in a very casual way, and my heart just hit the floor. She wants part of this. Why?

"Is that okay with everyone?" Maggie asks without even thinking. Everybody nods, except me. I don't know what this means. She looks at me, and I can see it in her eyes; she wants this. But what's this?

"Okay, it's settled then. I'll send the paperwork for you to sign. I'm out of here." Maggie politely smiles and goes. It's basically a fuck you all, I'm out. "I'll talk to you later," She whispers in my ear and taps on Olivia's arm.

"How much money are you talking about if I sell?" Leo asks. "Well, this place is valued at $436K, so we're taking about 85K roughly," Josh answers. Leo's face right now is priceless. He doesn't even understand this kind of money.

"Do you want part of this, or do you prefer to sell your part?" I ask him directly. "I'll sell, but only to you." He adds. If there's one thing I absolutely love about my siblings, it's their loyalty. "Done." Everybody nods.

"Well, you still have the majority of the shares. Are

you in, or will you buy all of us out?" Audrey is a pain in the ass, but a smart one; she is definitely our sister. I can't help but laugh. "I'm in." We talk about logistics, what we want to do with the place, the plans they have for the other two buildings, etc. And seeing Olivia like this—so focused, professional—somehow made me fall more in love with her.

CHAPTER NINETEEN

OLIVIA

I DON'T EVEN KNOW WHY I DID THAT.

This will absolutely complicate things with Ethan. Well, we already messed everything up, and this will definitely make it worse.

But the part of me that runs companies for breakfast, that loves a clean deal and a solid pitch, couldn't help herself. It's a great business opportunity, the kind that makes my brain light up the way my heart used to when I saw him.

We finished the night talking numbers, logistics, deliverables, and all the safe conversation we could have. The kind of conversations that keep the emotions out of the room. I take notes, ask questions, and lean into what I do best. The strategy, marketing, and control. Everyone seems pleased with the decisions and the plan. I'm nodding, smiling, pretending I'm fine.

Inside, I'm a mess.

When it's finally time to call it a night, Ethan catches me just as I'm sliding my laptop into my bag. "So..." he says, stepping closer, that crooked grin in place, "are we business partners now?"

I groan, tilting my head back. "Jesus, we're a cliché." He laughs, that quiet, low laugh that still hits me in the chest. "Could be worse."

"Could it?" I shoot back, but I'm smiling too. We leave the building together, the parking lot lit by the soft glow of streetlights. The air smells like asphalt and left-over rain. My heels click against the pavement, and his boots scuff beside me. It feels weirdly normal, which somehow makes it worse.

He opens the truck door, and I slide in without thinking. It's muscle memory by now, how easily we fall into old patterns. We start driving—no words, just the sound of the engine and the hum of tires on the wet road. I check my phone once, see a missed text from home, and put it face down on my lap.

Somewhere between one stoplight and the next, I realize I'm not heading home. I'm heading home *with him*. He didn't ask. I didn't say anything. It just... happened. Like gravity, pulling me in, same as always.

I should tell him to turn around.

I should. But I don't.

LAST NIGHT WAS WEIRD, in a good way. If you could say that. We didn't have sex. We didn't even kiss. Not once. We just... talked. Hours of it. About everything and nothing. About work, the kids, his mother's garden, and the first movie we ever saw together. We laughed at stupid things that probably weren't funny, shared stories we'd both already told a dozen times. It should've felt ordinary. But it didn't.

Somehow, it felt more intimate than anything else we could've done. There was no pretending, no heavy guilt in the air. Just the quiet comfort of being understood by someone who already knows every version of me, the best parts, the broken parts, the parts I try to hide.

At one point, I realized we were sitting shoulder to shoulder, watching the rain slide down the window, not saying a word. And for once, silence didn't feel awkward or forced. It felt safe.

And maybe that's what scares me most, that after all this time, after all the chaos and bad decisions, being near him still feels like *peace*.

Now, morning light spills across Ethan's living room. I'm curled up on his couch in one of his old t-shirts, and coffee in my hand. Trying not to overthink what has happened in the last two-ish weeks.

Ethan's across from me, hunched over his mug, turning it like he's searching for answers in the bottom. "It's been years," he says, voice low, steady but breaking around the edges. "And I still feel like I'm seventeen every time I look at you." My throat tightens. I stare down at my coffee, the swirl of it blurring in the cup. "Don't say that."

"Why not?"

"Because it makes this harder." He nods, slowly. "I know. But it's still true." I pull my knees up to my chest, trying to make myself smaller, maybe safer. "Some mornings, I wake up so sure. I love David. I do. I've built a good life. One that makes sense to everyone. But then you walk into a room, and it's like..." I stop, breath catching. "I forget how to breathe." Ethan runs a hand down his face, the sound of it rough in the quiet. "I don't think I've breathed right since the airport."

My chest aches. "This isn't fair."

"To them?" he asks quietly. "Or to us?"

"To anyone." He stands, crosses the room, and kneels in front of me. His hands land on my knees like he's afraid to grip too hard. "I'm not trying to wreck your life, Liv. I swear."

"But you are," I whisper. "Maybe not on purpose, but it's happening." He flinches like I hit him. "I have kids," I say, the words cracking. "A husband who's been nothing but good to me. Who trusts me." He nods, eyes down. "And I have Hannah. Two little girls who think I'm some superhero.

"So, what are we doing?" My voice breaks halfway through the sentence. His eyes find mine, steady and wrecked. "We're falling in love all over again." That's when I lose it. The tears hit before I can blink them back. Hot, fast, shaking. I press my palms to my face, but it's no use. It's not quiet crying, it's ugly, open, body-breaking.

He pulls me in, holds me like he's trying to stop the world from splitting. His arms are solid and familiar and the worst comfort I could want. "I never stopped loving you," he says into my hair. His voice is soft, almost a confession. "Not when you left. Not when I married Hannah. Not when my girls were born. I thought it would fade, but it didn't."

I look up at him through tears, blurry, broken. "I tried so hard to forget you." He touches my cheek, thumb catching a tear. I shake my head, choking out, "We can't keep doing this."

"I know," he says. "But I don't want to lose you."

"I'm not yours to lose." He exhales, a sound somewhere between a curse and a prayer. His hands find my face, holding me there, eyes burning into mine.

"You are mine. You always have been. And I'm not losing you again. I loved you yesterday, I love you today, I'll love you tomorrow and every day after that."

Something breaks inside me at that, the way he says mine, the rawness of it. Maybe it's that I still want to believe him, even when I shouldn't. I nod, barely. "We need to try to be friends. For real this time." He nods too, eyes closing like the words hurt to hear. We sit there, both of us quiet, both pretending that some peace might come from this.

Because we both know this isn't lust. This isn't nostalgia. It's the kind of love that doesn't go away. The type that ruins you.

CHAPTER TWENTY
ETHAN

WHEN OLIVIA LEFT, THE SILENCE HIT HARD. I sit on the edge of the couch, elbows on my knees, dragging a hand through my hair like that'll quiet my brain. Her voice still echoes in my ears. Her tears are still on my shirt. Every part of her is still here, even though she's not.

I love her. God, I love her.

And I love Hannah too. I swear.

Saying that out loud would make me sound like the kind of man I swore I'd never be. But it's true. I love the woman who built a life with me, who gave me two incredible daughters, and I love the woman I never really let go of, even when I told myself I had.

This pains me, and it isn't easy to accept. It's not supposed to be possible— to love two people like this. But here I am. Split down the middle. Bleeding out on both ends.

We keep saying we'll stop. Be friends. Reset. But we

don't know how to do that. Not when we just remembered what it feels like to have each other again.

And that scares the hell out of me.

LATER THAT EVENING, I'm seated on the porch, looking at the lake, at everything and nothing at the same time. And like any sane person, I open a bottle of whiskey and don't even mind grabbing a glass.

I drink from the bottle, and drink, and drink. Thank God nobody is here, because this is pathetic. *I* look pathetic.

I'm already buzzed, so I go inside and take a shower. I need that and to get some sleep. Water blasts my back, and the steam fills the room. It should help, but it doesn't. All I can think about is her.

My hand is on my cock before I even know I'm touching myself. The images hit fast, her legs wrapped around me, her breathy moans, the way her body opened up for me like she'd been waiting for it. Waiting for *me*.

My grip tightens, and I stroke faster. I picture her riding me, biting her lip, whispering my name like it still means something. I come hard. The sound I make is part relief, part regret.

I get out and towel up, just when I hear my phone buzz.

FACETIME INCOMING: HANNAH

My stomach drops. I'm too drunk to deal with this right now, and I'm feeling like shit. I pick up and see her. She's in bed, in a tank top, with no bra. Her cheeks are wine flushed. And that look in her eyes? I know it well. She's lonely, drunk, and horny. "Hey, babe," she purrs. "You look fresh out of the shower."

"Yeah," I say, playing it cool. "Just needed to clear my head." There's a pause. She nods, but her smile tightens. "Should I be worried about you being there with Olivia?" Oh, here we go.

"You're drunk," I say, softly. "Let's talk tomorrow." She doesn't push, doesn't say anything really. Instead, she slips her shirt off, fingers sliding down her stomach, and she starts touching herself. She knows sex has always been a way for us to communicate or to *avoid* communicating.

I watch her. I know shouldn't do this right now, but I do. I see how she stretches for me, I hear her moaning my name, I see her rhythm speed up. "Oh, Ethan, I miss you." Fuck, I do too. I feel all sorts of things right now, but this is my wife, the woman I've loved for the past decade. And without thinking, I start stocking myself again. Her breasts are bouncing, she's panting, wet. So, I let myself go. When I'm done, I feel bad, I feel guilty because even though she looks so good right now, all I can think about is Liv.

"I love you," Hannah says, voice barely a whisper. "Love you too," Is not a lie, but it feels wrong. And I end the call with a hole in my heart and my mind in shambles.

WHEN THE MORNING COMES, I'm restless. I can't stop thinking about her, wanting her. No matter how many times I try to stop myself from feeling this torn, I can't. I love Hannah, I do. But Olivia? Olivia's the part of me I never figured out how to live without.

I get up, brush my teeth, and lace up my shoes. Put on a hoodie, a hat, and get out the door. I don't text anyone. I need the silence today.

I run.

Through town, past the square. Every street is a fucking memory. The alley behind the hardware store, the library bench. The diner she used to work at. It's all *her*. This town is *her*. I don't stop until I'm standing in front of her house. The porch is still crooked, and the wind chimes are still singing like they remember me.

I stand there, breathing hard, like maybe the past will open the door and let me in.

CHAPTER TWENTY-ONE
OLIVIA

SUNLIGHT CUTS ACROSS THE HARDWOOD LIKE it's got something to prove.

And I don't need that today. My head's a mess. A full-blown, screaming, buzzing mess. My body aches, like heartbreak somehow decided to go physical this time. There's a heaviness in my chest that won't let me take a full breath.

It feels like I'm losing him all over again. The same hollow ache, the same quiet finality, except now we both understand exactly what we're giving up.

We need to be just friends, business partners, nothing more. We said all the right things adults are supposed to say when they're trying to be responsible. But it doesn't matter what we said. It doesn't matter what we feel. It doesn't matter because for a few days, we slipped and remembered what it was like to be us.

And it hurts. God, it hurts.

It hurts that I had to come back here— to see him, to

help, to play the part of the calm, capable version of myself, and instead, everything I was afraid of, just... happened.

All the years I spent stitching myself together, undone in one look, one laugh, one night. I press my palms to my eyes until I see stars, like maybe if I push hard enough, I can reset my brain, erase the ache.

I can't. I'm fucking miserable, and I need to go home.

MY PHONE PINGS as I'm debating whether to get out of bed or not.

> David: Haven't really heard from you lately. How did the business thing end?

> Me: It was good, I made a good deal out of it. Josh and Audrey are really good at business.

> David: Sounds like you'll kill it.

> Me: I'll know more after the weekend. But yeah... it feels good. Like maybe being here isn't a total disaster.

> David: I'm proud of you, O. Always.

> Me: How were the kids?

David: Wild. Matthew wore a blanket like a cape all afternoon. Declared himself King of the Backyard. Jer has been running behind him all morning.

Me: Ugh. I miss them so much.

David: We miss you too. Love you.

Me: Love you too.

I set the phone down. The guilt kicks in. He trusts me completely. And I'm breaking that trust in ways he hasn't even begun to imagine.

I get up and drag myself to the bathroom. The mirror's waiting for me— harsh lighting, no mercy. I turn on the faucet and splash cold water on my face until my skin stings, until the shock of it forces me to breathe.

When I finally look up, the woman in the mirror doesn't look like me.

Not the version my husband knows. Not the version I've been trying to be for years. This one looks tired. Hollow. A little ashamed if I'm being honest. I stare at her for a long time, waiting for the reflection to blink first. This is the version I don't want to admit exists, the one who still answers Ethan's calls, who still wonders what might've been, who's losing pieces of herself one compromise at a time.

I grip the edge of the sink, water dripping down my wrists, "What the hell are you doing?"

I head downstairs and stop cold on the last step. My stomach drops as I look through the window. "What the hell are you doing here?" I say as I open the door. He looks up, caught. "Hey."

"Hey?" I echo, my voice rough, caught between sleep and panic. He straightens but doesn't move closer. "I wasn't expecting you."

"I didn't expect to be here either," he says, rubbing the back of his neck. "Couldn't sleep any longer, so I ran, and ended up here." I let out a shaky breath. "Ethan, look, I get it. But we can't—" He cuts me off, and I swear I wish he hadn't, because I wasn't ready for what came next.

"I'm a mess, Liv." He looks at me like I'm a decision he already regrets making. "So am I, Ethan." He nods, eyes dropping to the floor. "I told myself I wouldn't come back unless I had the strength to stay."

"Ethan, you can't stay," I whisper. "Because I can't stay either. This—" I gesture weakly between us "—is bigger than just you and me. We have people we are responsible for, and we made vows to them long ago. And that doesn't vanish just because we are feeling all of this again."

He steps closer, just one step, ignoring what I'm saying. "Let me kiss you again, please," he says quietly. "Just once more, the last time." His hands come up to my face, palms warm, trembling. He holds me like I'm something fragile. His eyes search mine for permission, but I can't bring myself to give out loud. So, I stand there as he kisses me.

It's soft and careful. And it hurts, not in the way that bruises do, but in the way endings do.

It's the kind of kiss that feels like goodbye before it's even over. When he pulls back, his forehead rests against mine. Neither of us says a word.

We don't have to.

We both know this is the end.

CHAPTER TWENTY-TWO

ETHAN

I don't look back when I leave Olivia's porch.

If I do, I won't keep walking. I'll turn around and wreck both our lives. My lips still taste like her, but there's a sadness to it that I don't want. I can't remember her like this. Not again.

I make it home just as the town starts to wake. I drop my keys, pour coffee I don't even want, and stare out the window like the glass is going to hand me a solution.

Instead, my phone buzzes. Hannah. Of course.

I hesitate but answer anyway. "Hey," I say, already tired. "Did you see Olivia last night?" Oh, we're going right to it. No hello, no warm-up, just straight to fight mode. Today is one of those days that I don't have the energy to do this. I blink at my coffee like it might give me an out. "Oh, hi. Good morning, Hannah. Did you sleep well?"

She exhales sharply. "Yes or no, Ethan." I rub a hand

over my face. "No, Hannah, I didn't see Olivia last night. I was home last night. I was home long before you called."

"I'm going to ask you again, should I be worried about her?" I set the mug down hard. "Worried? No. We are just friends, we have a business opportunity with Josh and Audrey, I already told you all about this," She laughs, but it's clear that this isn't funny. "Oh, so you are friends now?" I grit my teeth. "We're trying to be." Silence.

"Do you still love her?" The words hit like a punch, even though I saw them coming. "You know the answer to that, Hannah. I told you a long time ago how I felt about her. I have never lied about that."

"That's not what I'm saying, Ethan. You still love her. This isn't in the past anymore, is it?" I don't answer right away. "That's not what this is," I lie. Fuck. What else could I possibly say right now? "No?" she says. "Because it feels like you're somewhere else every time we talk, and I'm not talking geographically."

"I'm doing my best, Hannah. I'm here because my mother died for fucks sake. I'm not here for fun. I didn't come here to see her or be with her. I came here to bury my mother, be with my dad and my siblings," I say, without even thinking, but it's the truth, and I'm sick and tired of this conversation. "So please just drop it," I say, softer this time.

She breathes in, sharp and shallow. "I know what you went there for, I'm not stupid. So okay, I'll drop it, for now." We hang up. No 'I love you', no nothing. I stand there, phone still in my hand, wondering how long I can keep pretending I haven't already split in two. Wondering if this is what it means to love two people, if it makes you rot from the inside out.

None of them deserve this, and I sure as hell don't deserve any of them.

I FINALLY SHOWER, throw on clean jeans and a button-down—and a little cologne. Grab my coat and head out the door.

We're meeting at the hotel site. Olivia, Josh, Audrey, and I have one big professional power hour where we all pretend something. The three of us are pretending to be the best siblings in the world, and the two of us are pretending we don't love each other.

The site's buzzing when I pull in. Josh waves me over, clipboard in hand. Audrey's already walking the perimeter with the foreman. "Glad you made it," Josh says. "Wouldn't miss it."

"We were talking about patio flow," Audrey adds. "Got time to weigh in?" I nod. And then another car pulls up.

Olivia steps out like she owns the place. She's wearing a cream blouse, a skirt that fits a little too well, sunglasses in her hair, and an oversized coat. She looks polished and sharp. Absolutely untouchable. She hugs Josh and Audrey. Then her eyes flick to me, just for a second.

"Hey," she says. "Hey," I murmur. This reminds me of the conversation at the airport, how stupid it sounded then, and how silly it sounds now.

We walk the site and talk logistics, finishes, and lighting. She drops into brand strategy like it's second nature. She is magnetic as hell, and I can't stop watching her.

"I'll be heading back Monday, but I can be on top of this during the week," she says casually, like she didn't just punch me in the chest. "Monday?" I repeat. She doesn't answer me. Something tightens in my chest. So I just nod, slowly.

Josh keeps it moving. "We need to have a follow-up in two weeks. There's a vendor walk-through. And I would like all of us to be here. Can we make that happen?"

"Sounds good, I'll be here," I say.

"I'll have the proposal ready by then," Olivia adds. We head back toward the cars. Josh and Audrey peel off toward their rental. I fall into step beside her. "Need a ride?" She hesitates on the porch, keys clutched tight in her hand like she's weighing every possible version of no. Then she shrugs. "Sure."

We slide into my truck. Doors shut. The sound is louder than it should be. For a second, I sit there, watching our breath fog up the glass. " So, Monday, huh?" I finally say, to fill the air. "Yeah," she answers, eyes fixed straight ahead. "I feel like it's time." Right. Time to go. Time to end whatever this was.

"And what happens with the project?" I ask, even though I already know. She exhales, the kind of long, tired breath that sounds like surrender. "I'll be in and out. I need to focus on work. But, I know that I can be an asset, so I'll help out." Her tone could freeze water. She's colder than the air outside, and it's twenty-nine degrees, so that's saying a lot.

"We should... take a break. From talking, I mean. Once we're back home." I grip the steering wheel tighter, but I can't look at her. Not right now. "You need space?"

"I think we both do," she says. "Clear our heads. Focus on our families."

"Right." I nod, staring at the windshield, the wipers squeaking against leftover mist. "Should we pinky swear on it? Or maybe we should have sex. Seal the deal properly." That earns me a smirk. She turns her head, just enough to meet my eyes. I blink. "Wait— what?"

She laughs. It's soft and unexpected. It's the first sound that's felt real all morning. "Relax. I'm kidding. Let's shake on it. You looked all serious and sad there that I had to make a joke." Yeah, right, a joke. She holds out her hand. Perfect posture, businesslike, detached as hell. I stare at it for a second too long before I take it. Her palm is warm, small, steady.

We shake, just like she wants. But what I want is to grab her, lift that pretty little skirt she has on, pull her panties to the side, and have her right here, right now.

But I don't. Because she's right, we both need space.

We both need to go home.

CHAPTER TWENTY-THREE
OLIVIA

Sunday evening shows up like a deadline I've been trying to ignore.

I don't want to leave. I feel like my mom still needs me, but let's be real, I've been using that as an excuse to stay for the past few weeks.

I know she is okay now, which means it's time for me to go.

I never intended to stay longer than a week, but everything with Ethan really messed up my plan. Between the will reading, the letter from Larna, and that stupid box, my mind is a mess. I don't even know what I'm feeling anymore. And that's the cue I needed to get the hell out of here.

I have so much on the line. My marriage, my kids, my job, the life I built back in the city. I can't put that at risk just because Ethan and I crossed a line— *multiple times.*

"Didn't notice you here." I'm so in my head that I didn't notice when Julia entered my room and sat across the bed. "I figure, so I just stare at you." She is insufferable.

"So, are you coming back soon? Or are you disappearing for years again?" Ouch, that hurt. I know she didn't say it in the way I felt it, but still. She's right. "Well, I'm working on the bar/hotel project, so I'll be back. Plus, honestly, Tacoon isn't as bad as I had in my mind for all these years." What I really mean is that my fear of seeing Ethan and being in the same place where he once left me is gone.

Which is a good thing because now I can see home for what it was before that, and for what it is now.

The only problem is that, now, when we're both here, the fear is gone, but the hope is alive, and that's a fucking lie. There's no hope for us, not in this lifetime at least. And I think that's just what I needed to realize.

"I'm glad you're going to be back. I've missed you. And you seem happy here. I can't wait for you to come with David and the boys." David and the boys felt like a punch. I nod and smile, "I've missed you too. And I don't want to be distant from mom anymore. I know she has you, Dad, and Anne, but it's not the same. At least not for me." And that's the truth. I've been so busy building my life that I excluded her, well, all of them.

I yank the zipper of my luggage, and it groans like it's in pain. And honestly, *same*.

I GRAB my phone just before my alarm goes off— 7:58 a.m. Late last night, I found an early flight, so I changed the one I had. This way, I can pick the kids up from school and maybe even surprise David when he gets back from work.

Mom's already in the kitchen when I go downstairs with coffee in hand. "Ready to go?" I smile and nod. "How are you feeling today?" She looks at me with such grace in her face; she's not hurting anymore, and that's a relief. "Honestly, I feel better. I miss her, and I'll always miss her, but I need to accept it and try to live with it." There's nothing I could say that can beat that, so I hug her.

Julia's not so far behind. When we're finishing up our coffees, she appears. "Oh, I missed coffee?"

"Don't worry, we left you some." We share some hugs, a few tears, and then I'm off.

THE DRIVE to the airport was quiet, but it's the kind where your brain won't shut up.

I move like I'm on autopilot. Carry-on, check. Bag,

check. I have my ID on hand. I'm grabbing a cappuccino I know I won't drink and a sandwich I won't touch. That's when I see him walking in. I didn't know he was flying out today, too. He's dragging his suitcase with one hand, backpack slung over his shoulder, and a protein bar in his teeth. Looking like some beautiful and infuriating disaster.

He spots me right away. "I didn't know you had an early flight." His mouth curves into that crooked smile that wrecks me. "I didn't. I found one late last night and decided to change it." He just nods.

"How are you feeling? I mean, about going back home after everything." It's an honest question, and I know he knows I'm asking about Larna and not us. We've been so 'busy' dealing with us that I haven't even asked in a while. "I'm good, being here kind of made me deal with it in a different way, a healthier way, I believe." I get it. It's the exposure to it all. I smile and nod. I don't want to drag out the conversation and force us to say or do something we don't need to.

"Well, I should get going, I board in a bit. Have a safe flight, Ethan." He doesn't look surprised by my change of subject or my sudden goodbye. He's used to this by now. "Yeah, have a safe flight, Liv. I know we promised not to talk once we're back home, but please, let me know you landed safely." I hate that I love him. I simply nod, because I can't keep promising things to him.

I start walking away from him, and it feels kind of poetic. We didn't have the chance to say a proper goodbye sixteen years ago, and today, we can finally say it.

"Liv," I hear it as a whisper, and I know I shouldn't look back, I should pretend I didn't listen to him. But then I wondered what he had called me for, so I turned.

"I love you," And that fucking wrecked me. Not because he said it, but because I feel it too. And I want to say back, God, I do, but I can't. I just can't. So, I look him in the eyes and smile at him. I know that hurt him, but I also know he'll be okay with that.

We must be okay with that. Because we need the distance. And because we have people waiting for us.

I keep walking towards my gate without looking back, just in time for them to call first class. And as I board that plane, I decide to leave him behind.

I love him, I will always love him, but this isn't our time.

We had our chance, and we'll always have that memory. What we just had was closure. To that chapter of us, hell, even closure to the whole damn book.

I need to see it that way, so it doesn't hurt more than it has to.

THE SECOND I step off the plane, it hits me hard.

It's not just the change in the air. That sharp, recycled city oxygen, it's everything around me. The noise, the lights, the motion. I'm not just back in the city. I'm back in this version of my life, the one that's supposed to fit, but suddenly feels two sizes too small.

Everything's too clean. Too quiet, too curated. The people in the terminal move with purpose. No one's looking over their shoulder, no one's falling apart. It feels fake, or maybe I'm the one who feels fake after everything.

The smell of coffee and perfume mixes with the echo of rolling suitcases. A kid laughs somewhere behind me. A man shouts into his phone about meetings and deadlines. It's all so normal, and I hate how much I don't feel like part of it anymore.

I spot my car right where I arranged for it to be, parked neatly in the long-term parking lot. I'm glad I asked the driver to leave it here. I need the drive home alone— I don't need the small talk today. I just need the silence and the low hum of the engine to drown out everything else.

The city is supposed to feel like home. But right now, all it feels like is the place where I have to start pretending again.

As I pull into the driveway, I spot David's car parked out front. Weird. It's barely one in the afternoon. He should be at work, buried in back-to-back meetings, late lunches, the usual chaos that comes with his job.

Unless something happened, but he would've told me. He always does. That's the thing about David, he's consistent and dependable to a fault. Predictable, in the best and worst ways.

Still, my stomach twists as I kill the engine. Maybe he

didn't say anything because he knew I had a flight today and I would freak out. I grab my bag, step out, and the familiar sound of the gate clicking shut feels suddenly too loud. The air smells like freshly cut grass and the faint trace of rain that hasn't fully dried yet.

Almost comforting.

I unlock the door, push it open, and kick off my shoes in the entryway. The house greets me in silence. Everything is spotless, the way it always is. The faint scent of lemon cleaner lingers, the kind of smell that usually means I'm home, safe, back in the life I built.

But today it feels off. Like someone pressed pause on it while I was gone. I drop my keys in the bowl by the door. The sound echoes down the hallway. "David?" I call out, but no response.

I head upstairs, still calling his name, thinking maybe he's on a call, maybe he's sick, maybe— that's when I hear it. A small sound. A rhythm that doesn't belong in this house.

Then his voice, low, breathless, unmistakable.

I stop dead at the top of the stairs. For a heartbeat, everything goes still— the air, my pulse, the world.

My body moves before my brain can catch up. I already know. A part of me has known since I saw his car in the driveway. But knowing and seeing are two different things.

I push the bedroom door open, and there he is. My husband, in our bed—*my bed*—with his assistant. For a second, my brain goes... blank.

She's on top of him, riding him, he has one hand on

her waist, pulling her hair with the other, she's moaning and screaming his name. The name of *my* husband. What a warm welcome home.

It's almost clinical, the way my body reacts. Everything slows down around me, my hands go cold but sweaty at the same time, and my stomach drops straight through the floor. I'm not even sure I'm breathing.

That's my bed. My life. And somehow, I feel like the intruder.

I don't know why I'm standing here just watching it. A part of me wants to scream and drag her down the stairs, another part of me wants to slap him, but I just *froze* there.

David has never even shown a sign that he might cheat on me. He doesn't even look at women when they pass by him. But everything comes in a flash. That night, when he was at his 'work dinner', I heard a woman's voice. It must have been her.

And that's when he sees me. She notices and tries to cover herself. Both were too stunned even to pretend it's not happening. Her mouth opens like she might explain it, like there's a single syllable that could make this better.

David's eyes go wide the second he sees me. "Olivia —" I laugh. It's sharp, automatic, not even real laughter, just something my body does to stop me from screaming.

"I was about to ask if I could join," I say, my voice too calm, too even. "But I didn't want to interrupt."

For a split second, no one moves. The room smells like perfume that isn't mine. She's still frozen, half-hidden behind him, wide-eyed and useless. I look straight at her, and she drops her gaze like a guilty kid caught stealing. I don't slam the door. I don't cry. I don't throw anything, even though a part of me wants to tear the whole place apart. I turn around and go.

He fumbles after me, yanking on pants, tripping over himself. "Olivia, wait—" At the bottom of the stairs, he grabs my arm. Instinct snaps in me, and I spin on him so fast his fingers slip off my sleeve like he's been burned. "Don't fucking touch me," I spit. He jerks back as if I struck him. "I, I— that's not what—" He stutters, hunting for sentences the way a drowning man grabs at air.

I cut him off before he can shape whatever lie he's been rehearsing. "Oh, you really are going to say 'that's not what it looked like'?" The words are a blade. "Because it looked exactly like you were fucking your assistant in our bed." My voice doesn't waver. I say it as plainly as I would say the weather, because naming it takes some of the power away. He goes pale. For a second, he's breathless, like someone pulled the air out of the room. "It doesn't mean anything. I swear it was just—"

"Just what?" I laugh, and the sound is little and bitter. "Just sex? Just a mistake? Because that makes it okay, right?" I can feel the blood in my ears. Everything goes narrow, and it's like my surroundings are just focused on him. "I want her gone now. And when I get back with the kids, I want you gone too."

He moves, like he thinks blocking the door will change where I'm headed. Like trapping me in this house will fix what he broke. He plants himself there, arms out, ridiculous and small. "Please," he says, voice raw, "just talk to me. Don't leave. Don't—"

"What's there left to say?" I ask, quieter now, and it's worse. The room seems to inhale. He meekly lowers his arms, like a man realizing the joke isn't funny anymore. He tries again, the same old lines he always used when something needed fixing, excuses, explanations, the cadence of somebody who's practiced being forgiven. None of it lands. I hear his words, but I don't feel them.

They're like a broadcast from a different planet.

My hands are shaking, not just from anger. From the way the world rearranged itself. I look at him, and I don't see the man who walked into my life. I see a stranger. I see how the father of my children just told me, with his actions, that our life was over.

"Get her out," I say. "Now." My voice is cold. The command fills the stairs, and there's no room for bargaining. I don't wait to watch what he does next.

I slam the door behind me and go straight to my car. And then, once I'm alone, I cry the whole way to school. I'm furious and humiliated.

And then I realize what a hypocrite I am.

I'm here putting David on the spot because he cheated on me when I've been doing the same for the past few weeks. What a joke. I'm such a fucking idiot.

I almost texted Ethan out of sadness and anger. My thumb hovers over his name. But I don't press it. I won't let this betrayal drive me back into someone else's arms. I won't make this worse.

The kids run to me like I hung the moon. I hug them

like I'm not shaking inside. We go grab burgers and milk-shakes, and I fake normal. Because that's what moms do.

Under the table, I text Julia. I explained everything, and she's as shocked as I am.

Julia: I'm here. I love you.

Back home, Beatriz is in the kitchen, stirring some-thing on the stove, humming under her breath. She looks up, surprised to see me this early. "Oh! You're home—"

"Yeah," I say, forcing a small smile. "We grabbed something on the way. But please, eat what you made. We'll have the leftovers tomorrow." She hesitates, but smiles, spoon midair, like she can feel the air shift before I even register it myself. "David's in his office," she murmurs.

The words hit like a static charge. Before I can respond, I hear him behind me. "Olivia." The house goes silent.

"Can we talk?" She scoops up the kids from the living room floor, murmurs something about bath time, and disappears upstairs without another word.

He steps into the kitchen, careful, like approaching a wounded animal. "I'm sorry," he says quietly. "It was a mistake. I didn't mean to hurt you." I lean against the counter, cross my arms, and look at him, really look at him, and for the first time, I see someone I don't recog-nize. "How long?" I ask. He blinks. "What?"

"How long has this been going on?" His mouth opens, closes. No sound. The pause is enough of an answer. "How long have you been screwing her, David?"

He flinches, but he doesn't lie. He knows better than that. "A few months, since February or so."

Something inside me shuts off. The pain is off, the rage is long gone, and I go numb. I've been beating myself up for the last few weeks, especially in the past few hours, thinking about how I'm a hypocrite and how we could work this out. Thinking that I could come home, tell him the truth about Ethan, ask for forgiveness, and try to move on. "Since February? Since your work trip to New York?" He nods.

"I want to know how this started."

"Olivia, I don't think that—" I stop him. "I want to know how it started." He sighs, "We were at the hotel bar after the conference, everybody said their goodbyes, and we just kept talking. She's been flirting with me since the company Christmas party, but I ignored it. She said she was into me, she got close to me, and kissed me. I know I should've stopped right there, but I just... Olivia, please."

"Keep talking," I know I'm just torturing myself right now, but I need to know. "She invited me to her room. I was drunk. I follow her and well."

"And well, what David?" Now I'm angry. He can seriously screw her in our bed, but he can't sit down and tell me what the hell happened? "What do you want me to say, Olivia?"

"The truth, all of it"

"I went to her room, and we had sex. We spent the night together and then, well, the rest of the trip too.

After that, we started seeing each other around. She was on every work trip I've taken this year, so yeah, it happened again. Happy now?" Something snaps in me. I decided in a split second. "Call my lawyer. We're getting a divorce."

"Olivia—"

"You made your choice months ago. I'm making mine now."

"You're ending our marriage over a mistake?" I laugh, sharp and ugly. "A mistake? You've been having an affair with your assistant for basically a whole year. You've been lying to me. You let her into our house. Into our bed. She was at the kids' birthdays this year for fuck sakes."

His jaw tightens. "And what about you?" he says suddenly. "If I have to guess, I'll say that you haven't exactly been a saint. Or am I wrong?"

"What's that supposed to mean?" Oh, now I'm angry. He is trying to spin this back at me. He is crazy. "You've been with your ex for almost three weeks, Olivia. You went out with him. There were nights you didn't call. I'm not stupid."

"His fucking mom died, David. Of course, I spent time with him. His siblings are my friends. My sister is one of them. What the fuck did you expect?"

"Not my wife spending time and getting drunk with her long-lost ex."

"Well, I didn't expect to come home and find my husband with his assistant bouncing on his dick and then find out he's been fucking her for a whole year. So, I guess we both expected something a bit different than reality, didn't we?"

I'm not saying a thing about Ethan and me. He doesn't get to know the truth now. He backs off after that, voice low now. "I'm sorry. That was out of line. Please— can we talk tomorrow?"

"You can talk to my lawyer."

> Me: Need to talk. Emergency. David cheated. I want to proceed with the divorce.

That night, I slept in the guest room. If you can call it sleep.

I stare at the ceiling for hours. My body is still on the bed, but my mind is screaming at me.

I grab some sleeping pills and roll over to the side. And let the numbness take me away.

CHAPTER TWENTY-FOUR
ETHAN

I TAKE THE WINDOW SEAT. PULL OUT MY LAPTOP before the flight attendants even get through the safety spiel. Dive into Tacoon plans like they might save me. I check the floor layouts and re-read the vendor lists. Check the permit timelines once more. I try to keep my mind on anything but her.

The flight attendant comes my way with a perky attitude and a smile, "Can I get you something to drink, sir?" Do they have something to erase someone from my mind? "Jack and ginger. Heavy on the Jack." She nods and smiles.

The flight was bumpy, which I'm glad, honestly, because between having to secure my laptop every five minutes and make sure I didn't spill my drink all over the keyboard, I didn't have time to think about her.

By the time we land, I've flagged half the blueprints and built out two fake timelines I'll probably delete and redo tomorrow. The phone buzzes as soon as airplane mode is switched off.

> Hannah: You landed?

> Me: Yeah, just now. I'll be home in a bit.

No message from her.

She should've landed a while ago. So this means we're done talking for good.

THE UBER SMELLS like mint gum and someone's cologne. The city rolls past like a screensaver. It is familiar, but it feels slightly off. Home greets me with glitter glue and chaos.

There's a massive "WELCOME HOME DADDY!" banner taped to the wall, complete with crooked stars and two tiny handprints in neon paint.

The girls barrel into me like they haven't seen me in months, and it surely feels like that. "Daddy! Daddy!" I drop everything, scoop them up, and bury my face in their hair. Hannah's watching from the stairs, arms crossed but smiling. I walk over, hug her, and kiss her.

"Welcome home," she says. It's warm, but I can sense she's mad about something, and she has every right to be. "You look tired," she adds as I set my bag down.

"Long day. Long week." She nods and, with no time to lose, she goes right into it. "Was it hard? Seeing her?" She doesn't say Olivia's name, but she doesn't need to. And I'm so tired of everything, the lying, the secrecy, so I go with it. "Yeah. It was." She takes that in.

"How's your dad holding up?"

"He is doing better than we expected. Maggie will be staying with him for a while." She nods, and I'm just waiting for the next blow. "I meant what I said on the phone," she says. "I know you're not fully here. And I know why." There it is.

"Hannah—" She holds up a hand. "Just let me ask you one thing. Am I waiting for this to pass again, or am I competing with her?" I lean closer to her. "You're not competing with anyone. I'm here." I kiss her, and I mean it. But she doesn't feel it the way I intended her to.

"I just need the truth, Ethan. Am I a placeholder?"

"No, you never have been." I chose her long ago, and by the time I started with her, Olivia and I were long over. Yes, I thought of her, yes, I loved her, but I never chose Hannah to forget Olivia. She gives a tight nod. "Okay." The nanny heads out to grab the girls.

Hannah gives her a soft thank-you, and I take my bag upstairs. "I'm going to shower. It's been a long day."

"I'll come sit with you." She perches on the edge of the tub while I strip and turn on the water. Steam curls around us. "How was the funeral?" I sigh, "Hard as hell. But it was a very nice service."

"And the project?"

"I didn't know what to expect working with them,

but honestly, that childish play we used to have is long gone. We're adults, we respect each other, and our parents' decisions weren't our fault. So, we're good, and they are professionals. We all are."

"Do you still love her, right?" I freeze. Water pounding my back. Eyes shut. "Hannah..."

"Don't lie to me, Ethan, please." And I don't want to lie. But I also don't know how to explain this to her. So, I settle for an easy answer and hope she takes it. "It's complicated."

"How so?" I guess she didn't.

"Can I be frank? No fighting, no nothing." She nods. "I love her, I always have loved her. She was a very important person in my life. And in a perfect world, I would have both of you with me. Because, trust me, I love you, Hannah. I chose you. I chose my life *with you*. And you gave me the two things I love the most in the whole world. But nothing erases what I had with her. I planned my life with her long before I knew you, and that's not something you just get over. I don't expect you to understand that I love two women, that I can have you both in my heart. But please know I love you."

She doesn't say anything. She stands there and starts undressing.

Without a word, she steps into the shower. Her arms slide around my waist, and I hold her and kiss her. She kisses me back like she's been dying to do so, her hand is in my hair, my hands are all over her, she's moaning, panting. She is my wife, and I owe this to her.

We ended up having sex right there, which is something uncommon. Hannah isn't the kind of woman to have sex outside of bed. She is very non-adventurous in that area, but the sex has always been amazing. And today wasn't the exception.

For the first time, I didn't feel guilty about what I told her or what just happened. Because even though I didn't tell her the whole truth, I answered her honestly.

The girls are coloring when we come downstairs. Dinner is chicken nuggets, glitter glue on the table, juice spilled, and bedtime chaos. Hannah catches my eye and smiles at me. I missed that smile. That one that says, 'everything will be alright'.

I'm home, I should feel whole, but something is missing, and I know exactly who it is.

BEING BACK at the office feels... off. It could be the jet lag. Could be the fact that I left half my soul somewhere between a motel bed and Olivia's front porch. Or maybe it could be that I was here when I got the news about mom.

I drop into my chair, crack open my laptop, and stare at a screen filled with unread emails. Project quotes. Vendor delays. Staff check-ins. Stuff I usually thrive on. But right now, it all feels like filler. Like a distraction I desperately need.

And then— ding.

ZOOM CALL – AUDREY, JOSH, OLIVIA.

My stomach drops. We said no contact, which means no calls, no texts, no catching more feelings. But this is business. And business doesn't count. I hit 'Accept' as I keep trying to convince myself.

Kara, my assistant, pokes her head in. "Moved your eleven to Thursday. Materials for Tacoon are confirmed. Want me to hold your one o'clock?"

"No, I need that one. Investor check-in." She disappears. I spend the next hour and a half hiding in spreadsheets. Nothing like numbers to keep you from spiraling.

At one o'clock, I log on. Audrey pops in first. Then Josh. Then— her. Hair pinned back, looking professional as hell. Something on her face is off, but she doesn't flinch when she sees me. Maybe the fact that we are supposed to be doing no contact or whatever the fuck that's called.

We dive into the call, discuss budgets, and talk about permits. Audrey talks about vendor quotes. Josh mentions some changes to the timeline. Olivia talks about strategy and marketing campaigns. She and Audrey discuss a few other things, and then the call ends.

Agnes walks in, taking me off my mind for a second. "Well, you look like shit," she says, dropping into the chair across from me. "Wanna get lunch, or should I fake an HR complaint to force you outside?"

I push back from the desk. "Lunch sounds safer." We hit the bar down the block. The place is packed at this time of day. I guess happy hour just started. It smells like whiskey and food. Heaven basically. We slide into barstools and order. A double for me, perks of being my own boss. I can drink in happy hour if I want to.

She narrows her eyes like she already knows why. "So, is this about your wife or the other woman you're emotionally combusting over?" she says, looking at my drink. I snort. "Both."

She sips her beer, waiting. She's always been patient with me. We met in our first year of college, after a sorority party I was forced to attend. She was the first woman I slept with after Olivia. And let's say that the sex was bad enough to never make us try again. Don't get me wrong, she is a beautiful woman, with the confidence of a pageant queen, and the attitude of a truck driver, in the best way possible. But we quickly discovered we were better as friends.

"Hannah keeps bringing up Olivia. Asking questions, like she knows something's off."

"Is she wrong?" She's staring at my soul. So, I keep drinking without looking at her. "No"

"You going to tell her?" I swirl my drink, still avoiding eye contact. "Eventually, I guess."

"You guess?" I glare. "It's complicated."

"Is it? Or you just fucked it up and now don't know how to deal with it?" I grin, because yeah, that's more accurate. "She doesn't know we slept together," I say. "But she knows what I feel about her."

"And the other one?" I catch myself smiling at the thought of her. "She's trying to pretend we can be friends. I'm trying to pretend I agree with her." Agnes nods, like she gets it. And maybe she does.

"I saw her the minute I got to Tacoon," I say. "It was like getting hit by a truck."

"Yeah, you look like that happened to you," she says dryly. "So, is she a truck you ran into willingly until you fell between her legs?"

"Fuck you," I mutter to her, laughing.

"Been there, done that, no thanks," she smirks. "But in all seriousness, don't be so hard on yourself, Ethan. You love them both, and that's okay. What's not okay is you cheating on your wife with your girlfriend."

"Okay, seriously fuck off." We laugh it out and keep talking about other things, because at this point, there's nothing left to do. I take a sip of my drink. "It wasn't just sex, Agnes. I can't even call it cheating. I love her, I'm in love with her. What we had never stopped, you know? I told Hannah long ago what I felt for Olivia, and I've always known I had love for her, but this was... is, something more." It just slipped out of my mouth, like I've been holding it for so long, because I have.

She exhales, long and low. "Jesus, Ethan." Then she asks the worst question ever, "Are you still in love with Hannah?"

I stare at my glass. "I... I don't know. I know I care about her. I respect her. I fucking love that woman. She's the mother of my kids. But, I don't know if I'm still in love with her. But I guess that even if I am, it's not in the same way I am with Liv."

Agnes leans back. "That's the thing, Ethan. You can absolutely love two people at the same time. But you can only be in love with one."

I stare at her and nod. "You've been in love with Olivia since you were ten years old. You almost didn't marry Hannah because of her. And now, here you are—married with kids, still looking at Olivia like she's the whole world for you."

"That obvious, huh?"

"Painfully." We laugh again, but this time it isn't as real. I sigh. "We agreed to take space. Focus on our families."

Agnes gives me a look. "And how's that going?" I ignore her and finish my drink. We talk about other things, like her love life, for once.

We joke around and go back to work.

CHAPTER TWENTY-FIVE

OLIVIA

THE SANEST THING I COULD DO WAS SCHEDULE a therapy session.

I already see Dr. Kamari once a month, preventative maintenance, emotional oil change, whatever you want to call it. And it's been good. Manageable. But this? This wasn't a "see you next month" kind of crisis. This was an emergency.

The office smells like leather and depression. Which feels fitting, considering I'm wearing both.

Leather pants, leather jacket, and what I can only describe as my best "barely keeping it together" perfume, equal parts heartbreak, dry shampoo, and existential dread.

I sink into the couch, the same soft brown leather that's seen me through every version of myself for the last three years. It groans under my weight, like it already knows what kind of session this is going to be. Dr.

Kamari sits across from me, calm as ever, legs crossed, notebook balanced on her lap. Her presence alone is unnervingly steady, as if she were built in a lab for people whose lives are falling apart.

I speak first because silence feels awful. "So," I say, voice too even. "My husband cheated on me." She doesn't flinch. She never does. Just nods once. "When did this happen?"

"Yesterday," I say, though it feels like years ago already. "Or maybe forever ago. Hard to tell." She tilts her head slightly. "Do you want to tell me what happened?" I laugh. Not a real laugh, more of a sound that escapes before I can stop it. "Do I want to? No. Do I need to? Probably." I stare at the floor for a second, at the way the sunlight cuts through the blinds in tidy little lines, making everything look organized, unlike my life. "I walked in on him," I finally say. "In our bed. With his assistant. Which, honestly, I didn't even think people actually did outside of bad TV."

Her expression doesn't change, but her voice softens. "That must have been painful."

"Painful, sure," I say, rubbing my temples. "And humiliating. And... weirdly predictable? I don't know. I can't tell if I'm heartbroken or just tired."

"Maybe both," she says quietly.

"Maybe," I echo. The clock ticks on the wall, steady and indifferent. "I haven't told the kids yet," I say. "And I don't even know what I'm supposed to tell myself. I spent years building this life— the marriage, the career, the picture of what happiness is supposed to look like. And now I'm standing in the middle of it, realizing half of it was fake."

Dr. Kamari leans forward slightly. "What do you need most right now?" I open my mouth, but nothing comes out. "I don't know," I say.

"I feel like an idiot." The words scrape their way out. "Maybe I ignored the signs. Maybe I wanted to." Dr. Kamari tilts her head. "What signs do you think you missed?"

I stare at the floor. The carpet's a soft gray, neutral and expensive, the kind of color that doesn't demand attention. "I don't know, when he wasn't home. When he was always... distracted. Distant." I let out a bitter laugh. "Apparently, it was just him being a cheating asshole." She doesn't react, not with shock, not with pity. Just that steady calm that makes people tell her the things they shouldn't.

"What else are you feeling?" she asks. I don't even hesitate. "I'm feeling guilty and ashamed."

"Why guilt?" And there it is. The question I've been circling since the minute I walked in. "Because I'm not exactly innocent," I say. My voice is quieter now. "I slept with someone when I was back home."

Her eyes stay on mine. No judgment, no surprise. Just space. "Someone I used to love," I add. "Someone I probably never stopped loving." The confession hangs there between us. It should feel catastrophic. It should crush me, but it doesn't. Instead, it feels like air finally filling my lungs again. For the first time in weeks, I can breathe. "I don't know what that makes me," I whisper. "A hypocrite? A coward?"

Her expression softens. "It makes you human," she says. "It makes you someone who was hurting and found comfort in someone familiar." The words hit something deep in me. Tears start burning at the corners of my eyes before I can blink them back.

"He reminded me of who I was," I manage. "Who I could still be if I wanted to." She nods slowly. "And now?"

I laugh, but it comes out broken, more like a cough. "Now I feel like I've wrecked my entire life. My marriage, my family, even my sense of self. And I don't even know if I'm mourning David or the version of him I built in my head."

"Both," she says quietly. "And that's allowed." That breaks me.

Because that's exactly what Ethan told me, almost word for word, and hearing it again makes everything blur. I look down, tears falling onto my hands, and I can't tell if I'm crying for what I lost, or for the parts of me I finally stopped hiding.

WHEN I GET HOME, I expect silence. I expect the

hollow echo of an empty house, the kind that matches the noise in my head. What I don't expect is Julia.

She's in my kitchen, barefoot, wearing leggings and one of my hoodies, the one she 'borrowed' years ago and apparently decided to make hers again. There's a box of muffins open on the counter and two sweating matchas sitting side by side like they're waiting for me.

I freeze in the doorway. "What the hell are you doing here?" She looks up, totally unfazed, and shrugs. "You texted. I booked the first flight out." That's all it takes.

Whatever fragile composure I was clinging to just snaps. I start crying, not the quiet kind, but the kind that hurts in your throat and makes you realize how long you've been holding your breath. Julia doesn't hesitate. She crosses the room in two quick strides and wraps her arms around me, tight. The kind of hug that doesn't ask questions, doesn't need context.

"I got you," she whispers against my hair. "Whatever happens, I've got you." It's simple, and it undoes me even more.

When I finally pull back, I'm a mess, red eyes, streaked mascara, puffy face. She doesn't comment. Just grabs a tissue and hands it to me like we've done this a thousand times before. "Did you sleep last night?" she asks.

"Barely." My voice sounds small. "So now what?" I exhale. "I don't know." She raises an eyebrow. "Bullshit. Try again." Typical Julia, blunt, relentless, but loyal as fuck.

I stare down at my lap, twisting a napkin in my

hands. The truth feels heavy, but saying it out loud feels lighter somehow. "I asked my lawyer to start the divorce." She doesn't flinch. Doesn't gasp. Just nods, slow and certain. "Okay, good."

Then she grabs my hand across the counter and squeezes. "You'll be fine." And that's it. That's all I needed to hear.

CHAPTER TWENTY-SIX

ETHAN

IT'S BEEN TWO WEEKS.

Two weeks since the Zoom call, since I saw her face pretending everything was fine when we both knew it wasn't. Two weeks of silence. Two weeks of pretending I'm not checking my phone every hour like a goddamn teenager.

Now I'm back in Tacoon, and the air feels heavier, maybe because it's colder, perhaps because I have new memories of her that hurt the same or more than before.

I pull into the site. Josh and Audrey are mid-convo with the foreman. I shake hands, nod when I need to, and pretend to care about floor plans. But I'm scanning the lot like an idiot.

She's not here.

When the moment's right, I ask, casual as I can, "Olivia not joining us today?" Audrey doesn't even look up. "She's around. Said she's handling some things. She'll jump in when she's ready." That doesn't sit right. Olivia doesn't miss things to handle others. She shows up, leads the damn room, and makes people listen. When the meeting wraps, I barely wait until I'm in the truck before texting her.

> Me: Hey, we just wrapped up. Surprised you weren't there. You were excited about this.

> Olivia: I'm back in Tacoon. Just handling a few personal things before I jump in. Everything's okay.

But it doesn't feel okay. That's not her tone. Not really.

> Me: I'm heading to your mom's house. I'll meet you there, and we can talk.

> Olivia: I'm not staying there.

> Me: Where then? Rental?

> Olivia: No. I bought a place.

> Me: Wait. You guys moved here?

> Olivia: Not we. Me. Well, with the boys. It's a long story.

That stops me cold. What the hell is happening? I stop thinking. I type.

> Me: Send the address.

Olivia: Ethan… I can't. I'm with the
boys. I'm dealing with some stuff.

Me: Liv. Send it. Now.

When the pin drops, I'm already driving.

THE PLACE IS TUCKED behind a line of pines on the edge of town. It has a hell of a view. You can see the city, the quieter side. You have pines all over it, and a lake at the back.

The front door opens before I make it halfway up the walk. She's barefoot, in jeans and a white tee, hair tied up. She looks tired but offers me a smile anyway. I walk inside. She shuts the door behind me. "What the hell happened, Liv?"

She doesn't stall. "David cheated on me." I stare at her, in total and complete shock. This motherfucker. "Wait, what? With whom? When was this?"

She rolls her eyes. "Yes. With his assistant. A couple of weeks ago, when I went back home. Any other questions?" My chest lights up with rage. "You're fucking kidding. I'm going to kill him." She snorts. "Get in line."

"Liv—"

"Look, I don't need a white knight, Ethan. I'm furious, I'm sad, and even a little ashamed. But I'm not a weak-ass woman. He cheated because he wanted to, and

179

he could. He chose someone who kept her calendar and legs open for him. I made my fair share of choices, too."

My fists clench. "Still—"

"No, Ethan." She steps closer. "I already yelled, broke some things, went to therapy, and moved out." I glance around as she talks. The space already feels like her— it's warm, sharp, a little chaotic, but alive. "So, you just... left?"

"I called my lawyer the minute it happened. And the city didn't feel like home anymore, so I came here, talked to my real estate agent, found this place, and I'm working on it."

"And the boys?"

"They're okay. Kids are more resilient than we think. They know we're starting over. I'll make it work." I look at her and feel like I'm seeing her for the first time again. She's on fire and holding it steady at the same time. "You should've told me."

"For what? I didn't want to be that woman. The one who shows up with her life in ruins, hoping someone will put her back together."

"I wouldn't think that." She looks me dead in the eye. "I'm not here to fall apart. I'm here to rebuild my life. And I didn't want to complicate yours. We had our thing, we talked about it. That's that."

"You're not a complication. You're—"

"Ethan," she cuts in. "Don't."

"Why not?" She sighs like she's tired of even thinking about this. And I don't blame her at all. "Because you're still married, Ethan, and I'm not. Because I made my choice to step out of a marriage where both people were in the wrong, even if only one got caught. " She exhales, eyes on the floor. "That doesn't mean this is some clean slate for you and me. This isn't a green light. This is me, rebuilding my life, being there for my kids." I nod.

She folds her arms, now looking at me, "I need space. To figure this out. For me, not for you, not for anyone else."

"I get it," I say. "But I'm not disappearing, not now." She finally softens, just a little. "Good, I appreciate that. But right now, what I need is a friend. Nothing more. If you can't be that, then we're done."

"Okay. I'll be that. No pressure, no nothing, just here. For you." She looks at me. Like, really looks. Then, in a whisper, "Thank you." And that melts me. I could kiss her right now and hold her. But I'll settle for a hug. I open my arms, looking at her, and she comes right in.

"You want to meet them?" she asks mid-hug. "The boys?"

There's a lump in my throat I didn't expect. "Yeah. I'd really like that." They are her kids, but also his, and a part of me envies him for that. He got to have her as a wife, as the mother of his kids, and he screwed that up. What a fucking idiot.

She lets go of the hug and walks towards the back-yard to open the door. "This is Ethan," she says. "He is Mom's friend." They wave. I smile. And in that moment, standing in the middle of her new life, I know something for sure. She doesn't need rescuing. She's already saving herself. I want to be around to see it all.

And maybe, maybe I'm finally seeing her as more than the girl I lost. She's the woman I'd do anything not to lose again.

CHAPTER TWENTY-SEVEN
OLIVIA

THE KIDS ARE FINALLY ASLEEP. MATTHEW'S curled into a tight little ball with his blanket over half his face, and Jer is spread out like a king in a twin bed, one sock halfway off. I stand in the doorway for a beat, just watching and breathing them in.

I don't think I've exhaled in days.

When I walk into the living room, Ethan's still on the couch. He has his glasses on, flipping through the floor plans Josh sent over. The laptop's on the ottoman. He's in work mode, but his eyes soften when he looks up.

"Do I look like a nerd?" he asks, tapping a corner of the page. I nod, laughing and dropping into the armchair. "I like it. This version of you," I say, signaling around the couch. I've never seen him like this. We barely studied in high school, to be honest, and I missed his college years, so this is new to me. And I like it.

He glances up with a smile on his face. "So now that you're actually here, you think you're in?"

"Oh, I'm in. A 100%," I say. "Still have a few contracts to wrap in the city, but I can manage most of it remotely." He looks at me, and I got the message. He isn't asking just about the project. But we both played it cool. He leans back on the couch. "Good. You'll be a hell of an asset."

I smile at him, but I'm secretly praying that he doesn't ask anything else. "Look at us. All professional and civil." He grins, then checks the time and stands, shrugging into his jacket. "I should head out. Got some updates to prep before tomorrow's walkthrough. And you should rest. You've been having long days lately."

I walk him to the door, and just as I'm about to open it, we hear footsteps on the porch. Julia barrels up, slightly out of breath, carrying a duffel and a giant tote bag like she's been on a month-long pilgrimage. She stops short when she sees Ethan. "Oh. Ethan. You are here."

"Hey," he says, polite but casual. "Long trip?" I ask, eyeing the luggage. "Only if you count the six-block detour because your street is blocked for god-knows-what," she mutters, brushing past both of us. He nods, then glances at me, something quiet hanging between us. "See you tomorrow."

"Night," I say. The door clicks behind him, and Julia immediately drops the bag in the entryway like she's claiming territory. "You brought the big bag," I say.

"Obviously. I'm moving in." I blink. "I'm sorry, what now?" She shrugs like it's no big deal. "You think I'm going to let you juggle divorce, two kids, a full-time job, an ex, and a crumbling emotional core all by yourself? Not a chance."

I narrow my eyes. "You're seriously moving in?"

"For a bit. Until you stop staring out windows like some Victorian widow waiting for her ship captain to come back from sea."

"I'm not—"

"You are. But it's okay. I'll keep the windows clean while you recover your life dramatically." I laugh, even as tears start slipping out. I don't want to cry again. This is not a breakdown. This is just a quick release. She wraps her arms around me, tight, no questions asked.

"You're doing it, Liv," she murmurs. "You're actually doing it."

"I'm scared," I admit into her shoulder. "I know," she says. "But you're also stubborn as hell and a lowkey badass. You've got me. You've got coffee. And like... six boxes of expired Lucky Charms in your pantry." I laugh again, because she's right, and also because it finally feels okay to.

"Thank you," I say.

"Always, that's what sisters are for." Later, we unpack. She steals one of my hoodies and tosses her bag into the guest room like it's hers now. We drink peppermint tea on the couch while the kids sleep upstairs, and for the first time in weeks, being here doesn't feel like I'm still grieving something.

I'm glad that Ethan showed up. I was hesitant at first, but I missed him. I know we're trying to be friends, but right now that's more than enough for me.

THESE PAST WEEKS have been tough. Settling in after so many years living far from here has been a challenge, to say the least. Between sending the boys to school, calls with the lawyers, visiting the project, and closing some things in the office, I haven't had much time for myself.

So tonight, I sent the kids with Julia to my mom's house, and I plan to take a bubble bath, drink a bottle of wine, and relax. I deserve this.

The water is hot, the bubbles are growing, the candles are lit. Perfect. I put my hair up in a bun and get undressed. This feels so freeing. But just as I put a foot in the water, I realize that I have free will and I can have a glass of wine in the tub instead of waiting to get out.

What's the worst that can happen? That I get drunk and drown? Life could be worse. At least my kids will be okay. This dark humor won't get me anywhere good. I need to talk to my therapist.

As I walk downstairs, I feel a cold breeze that I wasn't expecting, and as I walk to the kitchen, I freeze. "Eh, hey," fuck, fuck, fuck. What is he doing here?

"Hey, umm, what are you doing here? And why didn't you knock or call?" I can't believe this. He is staring at me, and I don't blame him. We've been trying to keep things friendly, non-complicated, and now I'm standing in front of him naked.

"Well, I knocked, and nobody answered. I saw the light was on, tried the door, and it was open, so I came in. Should I go?"

"No, no, it's fine. I was... Um, can you pass me that blanket, please?" I say signaling at the blanket on the armchair.

"Honestly, I would rather not," he says, smirking at me, and that's the moment I knew I had a choice to make. I could die of embarrassment, or I could play along. "In that case, take your clothes off." He looks at me, his smile is long gone, and now he seems confused. "If I have to be naked, so do you."

He thinks about it for a moment. I can see it in his eyes, and then he takes off his coat, and then his t-shirt. And he tosses it my way. "Put that on, it would look good on you." That wasn't my plan, but he is being smart, so I'll take it.

I put his shirt on and walk to the kitchen island. "So do you want a glass of wine, now that you interrupted my plans?"

"What exactly was your plan? Drink wine while waking naked around the house?" Ha ha, funny. "No, I planned to be naked and have a bubble bath while drinking the wine. But now that's ruined, and the water must be getting cold, so, do you want a glass of wine?"

"Oh, I can come upstairs, if you want. Not to be in the bath with you, but we could talk while you have your bubble bath time." He says, mocking me. Hmm, I think about that offer for about half a second. "Okay, let's go," I say, taking the t-shirt off and grabbing the bottle of wine. He stares at me, too stunned to speak. "Are you coming?"

"I wish, but I shouldn't," he whispers, smirking at me, but I hear him, loud and clear. I scoff, "Come on, nothing is going to happen. You can sit in the toilet."

We go upstairs, and I get in the tub. I know this isn't a good idea, but I don't want him to ruin my night, and he already saw me naked, so if he stays, and we drink wine, he'll know I'm wearing nothing but his t-shirt. This way, he also knows I'm naked, but I'm underwater and bubbles, so it's less tempting. I think.

"Fuck it," he says, undoing his belt and taking off his jeans. "Make room for me," I move and let him in. He sits right in front of me, legs open, so I'm between them, and he grabs the bottle out of my hands.

"So, what are you here for?"

"In your bathtub?" I roll my eyes at him. "In my house." He laughs at me. "I came to talk about the project, the new floor plan Josh sent over, and some other things. But I have a confession to make," he says between sips of wine, here we go. "What? And be careful of what you're going to say, Ethan. We're naked in a bathtub, and we're supposed to be colleagues and friends." He looks at me dead in the eyes. "I'm trying to act normal, like a gentleman and a friend, but all I want to do is kiss you since I came here."

"That was before or after you saw me naked?" I smirk. God, I really want him to kiss me and do whatever he wants with me. But I have to be strong. "Oh no, that changed the moment I saw you naked, and recently changed again."

"Changed to what?" I know I shouldn't be asking this— I know the answer—but I want to hear it. We can talk about it, but not act on it. We are strong. "When I saw you naked, I thought about every time I've had you naked lately," I sigh, "And now?"

"I'm not doing that," He smirks, and something inside of me starts burning. "Why not? Are you scared?" I'm almost crossing the line, I know. I should stop right here. "Yes, I'm scared."

"Tell me more." I'm staring at his eyes, but his mind isn't there. I can see him trying to fight this. "Now, I'm thinking about pulling you closer, wrapping your legs around me, spilling the wine over your body, licking every part of you..." I swallow hard. "And?" I say as I move closer, grabbing the bottle of wine from his hands.

"You know what can happen if you dare to spill a drop of that wine on your body, Olivia." It's like he is reading my mind. But I stop myself, because this is already way more than what we agreed on.

I go back to where I was and just keep staring at him.

CHAPTER TWENTY-EIGHT

ETHAN

I'VE BEEN STRONG FOR WEEKS.

She is tempting me so bad right now, and I've been here for her as a friend, as a business partner. I've kept my distance, but it's not easy. I just want to have her.

But no, she was just teasing me, and as soon as she took a step back, I breathed.

We stayed in the bathtub for a while, and we talked about the project, how the boys are adjusting to Tacoon, and how she is feeling. I don't even recognize us anymore. But this is good except for the fact that I've had a hard on for almost an hour sitting in this tub with her. But it's worth it. I get up, grab two towels, and help her out of the tub.

We wander to the living room, sit on the couch, and talk about everything, like we're the best friends in the whole wide world.

We finished our second bottle of wine in no time.

Between bad jokes and childhood memories, time passes quickly. After a while, she falls asleep wrapped around one of the blankets on the sofa. Her breath evens out quickly, soft against my skin. She's gone, out cold.

Me? Not so much. I lie there, staring at the ceiling like it has answers for me.

I love her. That's not new, and that's not the question. What's new is having her like this. I could get used to having this. And that's fucking dangerous.

I need to talk to Hannah.

I can't keep doing this to either of them.

AT SOME POINT through the night, we made it to the bedroom. I haven't slept with her in a while. But as much as I want, I can't stay here any longer. She might be mad at me when she wakes up, but I can't stay. It's already 6:10 a.m. when I gather my things, get dressed up quickly, and leave her a note

Had a great night, but had to run. - 8 E

Funny how my mind just remembered that we used to say '8' instead of 'I love you' when we first started. We were both afraid to say it, so we thought using a number would make it easier.

That was a nice touch.

Hannah called on my way home. It's way too early there, which can mean only two things. That she never went to bed or that she couldn't sleep. "Hey Hannah, it's early. Everything okay?"

"I just got home, so it's late for me." I knew it. I'm not going to fight about this. I know that she can be mad at me, but she's a great mother, and I bet my life right now that the girls are safe and sound at home. "And before you ask, the girls are with the nanny. I asked her to stay the night." Yep, knew it.

"Wasn't going to ask. I know you." She sighs on the other line. "Well, since you know me so well, then you know I called because we need to talk, and I've been thinking about some things." Which is code to 'I've been drinking, and I want to fight about everything.'

"Okay, go on." Here we go.

"I've been thinking, maybe it's best we take some space. While you're in Tacoon, I mean." I just got home, but I don't want to come inside and have this conversation with everyone eavesdropping, and by everyone, I mean Maggie. I sit down on the porch steps. "Okay, what does that mean?"

She exhales way louder than she is supposed to. "We keep fighting about everything. About Olivia, your new job, project, or whatever it is. About the girls. The fact that you don't want another kid. I don't feel like I know you anymore."

"I know, it's been a rough couple of months," I say,

but she just keeps talking. "I'm not asking for anything permanent. I think you need time. And maybe I do too." Now I'm the one who's exhaling dramatically. "So, what does that mean? For us?"

"It means for the next month, let's keep it about the girls. I'll try to give you some space, while I take some as well." There's a long pause. "You still love me?" She asks.

"I do", my reply comes instant, steady, because it's true. I do love her. She's the mother of my kids, she's been my wife for years, and my friend. There's love here. "But I don't think you love me the way you love her." She says, almost a whisper. I close my eyes. "I didn't say that."

"You didn't have to, Ethan. I know you— we have love for each other, but lately, love hasn't been enough. I know you won't be selfish enough to ask me for anything, so I'm giving it to you. The space, the freedom, the whatever you want to call it." I don't even know what to say. I know we've been fighting, I know she's not 100% happy, but I never thought she would ask or offer this.

"Hannah, look, I love you, and I want to—" She interrupts me. "Don't— don't treat me like a fool. I know you love me, but I need some space too. I told you I didn't want to be your consolation prize, and that's how I've been feeling lately."

"You're not that." She is not, but I can't keep lying to her. "Hannah, I—, yes, I love her, and she is going through a divorce right now, and I'm here, and she is here, and I—"

"And you want to be with her..." I cut her off and said, "And I want to be here *for* her. Look, I'm trying here..."

"Are you? Really trying?" She sounds pissed now, hurt. "I am. If this is what you want, what you feel like we need, then okay," She sighs but says, "Yes, I need to focus on me, because I can't keep waiting around for my husband to fall out of love with his girlfriend."

Oh, fuck she is pissed.

"Hannah, stop! She *was* my girlfriend, now she is just a friend." I'm lying to her, to myself. Liv is not just my friend. She is so much more. I was just in bed with her for fucks sake.

"Okay, Ethan, let's say she is your friend, and you want to be there for her. So go, be there for her. You have a month to figure things out, and I'll use it to focus on myself. If you want, I can fly the girls out there, and you can have them for the two weeks we were supposed to go there, but I'll stay here."

I don't even know what to say. She sounds so determined, and I should feel okay with this. I should have peace of mind right now. I should feel free, but I don't. Because while Olivia and I spend the night together, I know what she thinks and how she feels.

"Hannah, I—", she stops me again. "Ethan, I've made my decision, the one that I believe is the best for us. I love you, and you are my whole life, but I'm not yours. Take this month to clear your head. I won't ask questions. Let's just take a breather."

We end the call gently, I accept her terms, and we say our goodbyes.

I text Agnes a quick recap and ask her to check in on Hannah. She replies instantly.

> Agnes: Got it. Take care of yourself, too, idiot.

CHAPTER TWENTY-NINE
OLIVIA

WE'RE SUPPOSED TO GO TO THE BAR OPENING today.

Wild, really, how time flies when your life is falling apart, and you're trying to drown the chaos under spreadsheets and paint samples. It's been a blur of menus, marketing, invoices, and late nights.

If I didn't know better, I'd say overworking is my new love language.

I should be mad that Ethan left the way he did, no explanation, just gone, but I can't even find the energy for anger right now. Because yesterday changed things. *Again*. And not in the good, productive, 'we're two professionals getting stuff done' kind of way.

We've spent the last week pretending to be fine. Pretending to be friends, business partners, teammates. Whatever label feels the safest on any given day.

We built this bar in record time, and honestly, it looks incredible. It's the one thing in my life that doesn't feel like a disaster right now. So why does it still feel like standing next to him is lighting a match in a room full of gasoline?

We shouldn't put everything at risk just because we enjoy being naked around each other, which is a ridiculous sentence, but an accurate one.

The problem is, I can't decide if being near him feels like comfort or self-destruction. Maybe it's both.

I'm divorced now. Officially. Done. Paperwork signed, ring in a drawer, lawyer paid. He isn't. Not even close. And I know what that means. It means the line has to go back up, sharp, bold, permanent.

No blurred edges, no excuses. We need to stop pretending we can hold the fire without getting burned.

THE BAR IS BUZZING when I walk in. The industrial lights in the ceiling look great, and the polished wood counter adds a nice touch. And those soft amber bulbs are to die for. We did good. Very good.

Everyone has gone to mingle, even though we've been here for barely five minutes. I stay behind and wait for Ethan, who just walked through the doors. "You okay? You look like a sad puppy." He shrugs.

He rolls his eyes at me. "Hannah and I are taking some time apart while I'm here in Tacoon." Oh shit. I wasn't expecting that when I made the joke. "Is this because of me?" His brow furrows. "Not just you," he shakes his head, and I let out a breath.

These days, I don't know what he says to her and what he chooses to keep to himself. I know he's not going to tell her we slept together, but he might say enough for her to spiral. And I don't blame her, how could I? I feel bad for her. I feel bad for him. This isn't an ideal situation, and I know I'm in the wrong on this one. *So wrong*.

"But yeah, part of it is. She thinks I'm still in love with you." Oh, I swallow hard. "Are you?" He let out a short laugh. Sounded like a bad joke, but it is an honest question. One thing is to love someone, and another to be actively in love with that person. "I didn't have to say it, she knows. It's written all over me." I lean in slightly, "Oh Ethan..."

"I'm not asking for anything," he whispers. "But I needed you to know—"

"For what, exactly? So, I don't feel bad that we spent the night together. Why do I need to know that you and your wife are taking time apart?"

"Because I needed you to know that I'm here, Liv. I'm here *for you*." I just stood there looking at him. "Say it, Liv." I bite my tongue. I can't say it. "Ethan, I... I don't know what to tell you. What does this mean for you? For us? Is there even an '*us*'? I'm just confused." I take a breath and look away.

"This means I'm here. I'm not going anywhere unless you ask me to leave. It means that I love you. That I'm *in love with you*. And Hannah knows it. It means I have a whole month to figure out if you feel the same. If you still feel what I feel." I'm suddenly speechless. This is what I wanted to hear, but it doesn't feel like that. Not anymore.

"Ethan, this is not the best time for me to help you figure things out. And it's not the time for me to even *want* the idea of us." I sigh, frustrated, not at him, at all of it. The timing, at how much I've already lost.

"Liv, that's the point. There's no idea of us. There is an *us*. We're right here."

"I'm not your hall pass, Ethan. You can't just say you're taking a break from your wife and expect some sort of free trial for a month with me." Fuck, I can feel my eyes fill with tears.

"Liv—" His voice breaks, but he tries to hide it. "This is not that. You're not a hall pass. You're not a free trial. For fuck's sake, you're not temporary. You are it. I fucking love you. I've been in love with you since I was ten years old. You were—" He chokes, and I just start crying. "You *are* my everything." Now I'm really crying.

He takes a step closer, way closer, and he kisses me. It felt like he was oxygen, and I needed to breathe.

And when the kiss finally breaks, we're both panting. "Are we really doing this?" He nods. "We need to get out of here. Now. My place."

He blinks, "What about the boys?"

"I'll text Julia. She'll take them to my mom's and stay the night."

"Let's go." He grabs my hand, tight, and we leave the

bar like we're running from something, or towards it. Either way, we don't look back.

THE DOOR HAD BARELY clicked shut when he had me. He didn't hesitate. He backed me into the wall like he couldn't breathe without touching me, his mouth crashing into mine, his hands already in my hair, gripping like he'd been starving. I kissed him back just as hard.

His hands were everywhere. By the time we stumbled into the bedroom, I was in nothing but my underwear, and he was just muscle and heat. One look in the mirror and I nearly lost it. We looked wrecked already.

Two people devouring each other like they were running out of time.

He grabbed my thighs and lifted me. I wrapped around him, holding on as he pressed me into the wall again, his mouth on my neck, one hand on my ass, the other sliding under my bra. He dropped me onto the bed, staring at me like I was something he hadn't let himself look at too long. "Spread your legs."

His voice was rough. There was no patience there, just a need. So I did as he told me.

His hands slid up my thighs, his breath brushing me before his mouth did, and then I was gone. His fingers were in me, and I couldn't stop moaning. "I need you to be mine, and not just for tonight."

My hands grabbed his hair, the sheets, anything solid I could find as I came. It was loud, hips shaking against his face. He didn't stop. He wanted every last drop of me. He stood up, started stroking himself as he watched me breathe. So, I dropped to my knees and took him into my mouth. His hands tangled in my hair, guiding me. "Liv, fuck, don't stop."

I couldn't have if I tried. He throbbed on my tongue, his voice breaking as he said my name repeatedly. Then his hips jerked, and he was finishing, hot down my throat. I swallowed every drop because I could, and more so, because I wanted to.

He stared at me like I'd just knocked the wind out of him. "Jesus, Liv. What am I supposed to do with you?" His voice wasn't demanding anymore. It was pleading.

And I knew exactly what I wanted him to do next.

CHAPTER THIRTY
ETHAN

SHE'S LOOKING AT ME LIKE THIS IS FUN FOR HER, like she wanted this side of me. She's not scared. She's amused, almost daring me to keep going. She laughs once, nervous and breathless, and the sound cuts right through me.

For a second, I see past it, the front, the control, and there's something small and breakable underneath.

I grab her thighs with one hand, and with the other, I grab one of her breasts and start playing with her nipple. She is soaked, clutching the bed, and gasping for air. Then I stop. She lifts her head, confused. "Ethan, what the hell—"

I don't answer. I look at her and grab her by the neck. I slide two fingers inside of her, and she fucking loses it. She whimpers. "Oh, fuck." She's trembling, her back arches, hips rocking against my hand. I press my palm against her, curl my fingers, and she's shaking again.

I stop when I feel she's almost done, grab her thighs,

and put my mouth on her. She's squirting like she's never done before. She is a mess. She's soaking wet, her eyes are watery, unfocused, like she's caught somewhere between wanting to speak and forgetting how.

She's trembling, breath coming fast, every inhale uneven. She is flushed, but she wants more. I can see it. "I can't even think right now," she says, her voice rough and low.

"On your knees, face down. I want your ass up." She hesitates.

"Now, Liv." She shifts, and I guide her into position, one hand steady on her hip, the other sliding between her shoulder blades. And then I'm inside her, deep, slow, all the way in.

I grip her wrists behind her back, controlled, firm, but careful. "You take me so well, Liv." She moans again. I set the rhythm, hard and deep, and she meets every thrust like she wants to burn this moment into her spine. I lean forward, pull her up so her back hits my chest, and wrap an arm around her waist.

Fuck, this woman is fantastic.

"I'm about to finish, Liv, and I won't stop until you're filled." She nods and lets herself go into my arms. I hold her close while I finish inside of her.

This is the most amazing sex we've had so far.

CHAPTER THIRTY-ONE
OLIVIA

BEFORE I CAN EVEN CATCH MY BREATH, HE FLIPS me onto my back, and he starts touching me again, gently this time, and I'm just scratching his back and pulling him closer to me.

It's the best sex we've ever had. No contest.

We take a breather for a moment, as he is on top of me. We're just there, gasping for air. We don't say anything, but we're feeling everything.

Even though I'm tired, because this has been an exhausting, passionate, fantastic night. I push him so he's next to me in the bed, and I climb on top of him.

I start kissing him, he's grabbing my breasts, I'm holding his hair, we are sweaty, and it's messy, and I can feel he's getting hard again, and I start grinding on him. I grab him with one hand, and I tease my entrance with it.

He's smirking now, eyes gone dark. "Liv—" I start riding him slowly in circles, and he's losing it. Then, a bit faster, and he snaps. He pulls me in, shifts us so I'm straddling him upright, face to face, one hand in my hair, the other on my hip, grounding and guiding me.

My nails rake down his back. His mouth is on my neck. We're both loud now, cursing, begging, promising shit we probably shouldn't. I ride him harder. Faster. It's filthy and perfect.

And we're both done.

We stay there, he is still inside of me, we're just kissing slowly. Eventually, he pulls back just enough to brush a few strands of hair from my cheek, his eyes searching mine with something like wonder.

"You, okay?" I nod, smiling through the haze. "More than okay." He chuckles, low and warm. "Good. Because I was about to call that the best sex of my life, and it would've been awkward if you were, like, 'meh'." I laugh at him. "You really know how to ruin a moment, don't you?"

"Top-tier talent," he says, kissing my forehead. When we finally untangle and get up. "You hungry?" I ask as I walk to the bathroom. "Starving. But please don't tell me you're one of those people who have, like, chia seeds and expired almond milk." I laugh. "Worse. I have two frozen pizzas. Shaped like dinosaurs? Courtesy of Matthew and Jeremiah."

"Perfect," he says. We wander to the kitchen. The oven hums to life as Ethan preheats it. I sit on the counter, legs swinging, watching him. "You know," he says, pulling the pizza boxes out, "There's something poetic about us eating dinosaur-shaped food at 3 a.m."

"Don't overthink it. We're survivors. The dinos

weren't." He grins and points a plastic spatula at me. "That was dark."

The pizzas go in, and a few minutes later, we're curled up on the couch, plates balanced on our laps, trying not to burn our tongues. I glance over at him. His bare chest is still flushed from what just happened. He looks at me like he doesn't want to blink. "What?" I ask, cheeks warming. "Nothing," he says. "Just taking it all in."

"Me too." And we eat in silence for a while.

Two Weeks Later

It's been a week and a half of... *us.*

The days are starting early now, with coffee in bed and morning sex. I'm trying not to get used to it. But God help me, I am. We haven't labeled this thing. We have no expectations.

And while a girl can dream, the reality always creeps in.

I have to admit that I can see something in the way he brings me Sour Patch Kids from the gas station, just because he was thinking about me, the way his hand finds mine when no one's watching. The way he acts like my kid's crayon drawings belong to MoMA.

This no longer feels like teenage love. It feels like we have outgrown every bad thing that has ever happened to us, and now we can be a better version of ourselves. But under all the good— because yeah, it's good—there's this thing I keep stuffing down. What happens when this month ends? He hasn't brought it up, and neither have I. Maybe I'm just scared that the answer is precisely what I don't want to hear. Because right now, when he looks at me, it makes sense, but at the end of this month, he might look at me differently, and I'm not ready for that.

I still wake up some mornings with that sharp, empty feeling. We started this because we were grieving Larna together. And while grief doesn't pack its bags and leave overnight, the sad part of it is over.

Now, we find ourselves talking about her peacefully, no tears, just happy thoughts. Everything feels a bit lighter these days.

I'm liking my life right now. I'm spending more time with my mom, Julia, my dad, and even Anne. They get to see their grandkids, and for the first time in a while, Tacoon feels like home again.

I went to my mom's house to pick up the kids, and Julia is giving me the 411 on her latest date. I love how easy her love life is. I envy her, really. She's been 'dating' this girl, even though she doesn't believe in labels. I can see she really likes her. She's happy. I'm happy.

A text comes up, and I find myself laughing at my cellphone. It's been a while since I felt this way.

> Ethan: Miss you. Withdrawal's real.
> Can I come over?

> Me: Just picked up the kids, and Matthew's not feeling great. I'll have a cozy night in with the boys. Rain check?

Fifteen minutes later, he shows up with soup, electrolytes, crackers, Legos, and a bottle of wine.

We built some strange figure I can't decipher yet, we play cards, and cuddle under blankets. The boys giggle at his dumb voices. My heart does this stupid thing where it skips a beat and then beats faster than ever. I might have a heart problem now that I think about it.

Maybe it's the father figure in him, perhaps it's the love he has for me, and for them. But watching him being so parental does something to my ovaries.

Later, as they fall asleep, his phone lights up. It's her.

> Hannah: Do you want the girls to fly out next week?

He shows me the screen. I nod. "The boys are going to David's next week. If you want them to come, you'll have space. I can help, but only if you want me to meet them." I say.

He exhales, eyes searching mine. "You'd really be okay with that?" Am I okay meeting their children? Absolutely not. I don't know how I am going to feel, much less how she is going to feel bout this. About knowing I met her girls. But if I'm in his life, I guess this is bound to happen. "I'd love to." If she agreed to this month and us being together, she must know. As a woman, I get it, but as a mother, I'm terrified.

208

He texts Hannah back. We settle on the couch, the kids asleep around us, our hands linked.

Whatever this is, it's becoming something real.

CHAPTER THIRTY-TWO
ETHAN

THE PHONE BUZZES JUST AS I'M FINISHING MY coffee.

HANNAH

I stare at the screen longer than I should before picking up. "Hey."

"Morning." Her voice is calm, too calm. That tone she uses when she's trying hard not to sound like she's bracing for something. "So, I talked to Agnes," she says. "She can't bring the girls. She's flying out tomorrow for a work trip." I rub the back of my neck. "Okay... so what's the plan?"

"I thought I'd bring them. I can fly in and out the same day." My stomach tightens. The idea of having both Hannah and Olivia in the same place at the same time is not great. It can become messy quickly. "Hannah, that's a long-ass day. I won't let you put yourself through that."

There's a pause, "I figured you'd rather I didn't show up at all."

"This isn't about us," I say. "It's about the girls." And I mean it. "Bring them," I add. "But don't rush back. You can stay the night and take the morning flight the next day."

Another beat. "Okay," she says. "I'll book it."

After we hang up, I text Olivia.

> Me: Hey. Update. Hannah's bringing the girls. She'll stay the night and fly out the next morning. Just keeping you in the loop.

> Olivia: Thanks for the heads-up. I'm slammed with meetings, but come by later?

> Me: Bringing wine.

My next call is with Audrey. She's still out of town sourcing for the hotel. "We got the reclaimed wood," she says, all business. "Good texture, warm tone, matches your moody-ass Pinterest board." We run through supplier timelines, lobby layout tweaks, and punch-list items. She's excited. I try to keep up.

Phone buzzes again—

AGNES

"Hey, trouble," she says. "Sorry, I really wanted to bring the girls, but I'm slammed."

"No sweat. Hannah's coming instead."

"Oof," she says, and I can hear her wince. "You good

with that?" I lean back in my chair. "Not thrilled. But it's fine. I haven't seen them in two weeks. I'll take what I can get."

"You want me to fly out after my trip?" she asks. "Keep you sane? Bring snacks? Judge your life choices in person?" I laugh. "Actually, yeah. You can finally meet Olivia." There's a beat of dramatic pause. "Oh, I've been waiting for that. Count me in."

By the time I pull into Olivia's driveway, the sun's already going down. She's at the dining table, hair piled on her head like it's holding her brain together, typing like she's running out of time. I drop my keys, walk over, and gently shut her laptop.

She blinks up at me. "Hey."

"Yeah, no," I say, already grabbing the wine bottle and two glasses. "You've been doing this all day. You need air. Blanket. Stars. Me."

Five minutes later, we're on the back porch, under that old quilt she never actually washes. The sky's clear. The wine's cold. Her body's warm against mine. "I heard from Hannah," I say, eyes on the sky. "She's flying in with the girls tomorrow." Olivia doesn't flinch, sips her wine. "Okay."

"You sure?" She sighs. "I'm dealing with enough of my own crap," she says. "She's your wife. I'm not here to make it harder."

"But this—"

She shakes her head. "Don't. We don't need to talk about it. Not tonight at least." She leans into me. I kiss the top of her head, then her temple. She turns to me, and that's it. We're kissing, and it feels like the world just went quiet for us.

She gets on top of me, shifting her hips over mine. The blanket slips slightly as she moves again, rolling her hips in a way that makes me grip her tighter. My head falls back against the wood. She leans forward, mouth trailing down my neck, her hair spilling over my shoulder like silk. "You're driving me insane," I groan.

I pull the blanket tighter around us, like we can trap this moment and never let it go. My hands roam over her bare back, the swell of her ass, the soft press of her breasts against my chest. Every inch of her is mine and not mine at the same time.

She grabs me, eyes locked on mine, and guides me to her entrance, already soaked, ready for me. I groan, low and broken, and grip her hips as I pull her down onto me in one swift thrust. We both gasp. God, she feels so fucking good stretching around me. Her forehead presses to mine as she starts to move. She rides me like she wants to feel every inch, every pulse. Our mouths are open but wordless, breath catching between us, broken only by the quiet sound of her moans.

She picks up pace, grinding faster, and something in me snaps. I flip her onto her back, blanketed beneath me, and drive into her, hard, deep. She cries out my name, "Ethan—," breathless, wrecked. "Be quiet, Liv," I whisper against her neck. I grab a pillow from the couch and slide it under her hips, lifting her just enough. I start to move, slow at first, working on my pace. She moans again.

"Liv," I warn, my voice low and sharp, "I said quietly. I don't want to hear a sound." She nods quickly, lips parted, already trembling. Her body quakes beneath me, her moans caught in her throat, her fingers twitching in my grip. As she finishes, she stays quiet, just like I told her.

But her eyes scream everything I already know.

She's mine.

The house is still dark when I slip out of bed, Olivia curled into the pillow. Her hair's a mess. She looks peaceful. Which is dangerous, because I'm getting used to this. I tug on sweats, pad into the kitchen, and start breakfast. Pancakes. Eggs, I'll probably screw up. Coffee, because we're both useless without it.

She walks in a few minutes later, eyes sleepy, hair everywhere, wearing one of my t-shirts.

"Morning," I say, handing her a mug. She leans in and kisses my jaw. "You're cooking?"

"Trying to," I mutter. "No promises on the eggs." We eat in silence and then get ready for the day. She stays behind, and I head to the site for a check-in with Josh. It's the usual: timelines, delays, Audrey's notes from her latest design deep-dive.

By NOON, I'm standing in the terminal. Then I hear it

— two high-pitched voices scream "Daddy!" and it's game over. I drop everything.

They crash into me, arms wrapped tight, little faces pressed to my neck. I haven't seen them in two weeks, and it feels like years. Hannah follows behind, dressed in jeans and a soft sweater, looking good, happy like she's fine. Like we're fine. "Hey," she says, pulling me into a hug. Her cheek brushes mine as she kisses the corner of my mouth. "Hey," I say. "Flight, okay?"

"Easier than expected." She bends to fix one of the girls' jackets. "Thanks for letting me bring them." We grab lunch downtown. The girls are full of stories—new swings at school, a boy named Colin who only speaks in a robot voice. Hannah talks about her job at the gallery and how it feels good to build something of her own. And I listen. I really do. I'm proud of her.

But it all feels... far.

Like I'm watching someone else's life from the outside.

BACK AT MY dad's house, he whisks them off on a made-up 'treasure hunt', and I catch Hannah watching him like she's remembering a time when this felt easier.

Later, I hear the shower shut off in the guesthouse. Hannah walks out in leggings and a black tank top, hair wet, skin glowing in that familiar way that used to stop me in my tracks. I still notice. Of course I do. I'm not blind. She's beautiful, and she is my wife. And this part of my life? It still exists.

This love doesn't just vanish because we're figuring things out.

Dinner was great, Maggie showed up. The girls are running barefoot in the yard. It's easy. This version of life is the one I used to know.

After, I help Hannah bring the bags into the guesthouse. "You sure you want to crash in Leo's room?" she teases. "This feels like punishment, just sleep with us." We arranged the storage room so they could stay here, with two twin beds and a tiny nightstand.

Hannah is putting the girls to sleep, and I can hear them fighting even though they're exhausted. I'm in the other room in bed, going through emails and tomorrow's to-do list. "They are finally asleep," she let out an exhale and dropped to the bed next to me.

She rolls toward me, fingers brushing my shirt. "Did you miss me?" And of course I did, I do, every day. "Yeah," I whisper. "Of course I've missed you." Then she kisses me. But she's guarded. It's like she's asking for my permission to kiss me. And for a second, just a split second, I let her, and I kiss her back.

I love this woman, and in a perfect life, I could have both of them. But in reality, I know I can't, so just before the moment it gets more intense, I stop. I press my forehead to hers. "I can't." She pulls back just a little, eyes glossy but steady. "I'm sorry."

"No," I say. "Don't be. It wasn't just you. It was both

of us." I sit up. Swing my legs over the side of the bed. "It's just that I don't want to mess things up. You asked for a break, and I'm trying to respect that. I'll take the couch." She nods. "Okay."

The couch is too small. The cushions suck. But I lie down anyway and stare at the ceiling.

Everything aches. But I made the right call.

I WAKE up with a stiff neck, the sunlight stabbing through the curtains like it has something to prove. I groan, sit up slowly, and try to remember what day it is. What version of me am I supposed to be?

When I make it into the main house, the girls are already up, mid-bite, cereal all over the table. Hannah and my dad are laughing like this is just some Tuesday morning in 2018. Maggie's just walked in, bag dropped on the floor, animated as hell.

"You look like you fought the couch and the couch won," Hannah says, amused. She's not wrong. "It did." She hands me the cream. Her fingers brush mine. "I was just telling Maggie that my flight's at four. Thought maybe we could grab a late lunch before I go?" I nod, clearing my throat. "Yeah, sure. I've got a site thing with Josh this morning, but I'll be back in time."

"Great." She smiles. "The girls would love that." I sit there for a few more minutes, nodding at whatever

Maggie's talking about. But my head's already halfway across town.

I text her as I pull up to the boutique hotel.

> Me: Headed in. Need me to pick you up?

> Olivia: Already on my way. See you there.

She rolls in five minutes later in a navy dress, cream coat, hair windblown, coffee in one hand like she owns the damn day. She steps out of her car, and I don't even hesitate— I walk right up, wrap my arms around her waist, and kiss her.

She melts into it for half a second, then pulls back, blinking like I short-circuited her. "What was that for?" She watches me for a beat. "You, okay?"

I almost tell her. About last night. About how Hannah kissed me, how I kissed her back before pulling away. I nearly say the thing I haven't admitted out loud, that I'm confused as hell, and tired, and the guilt is eating me alive.

How is it that I feel guilty for kissing my wife, but I don't regret a single thing that has happened with Olivia? This doesn't make sense. But love doesn't have to make sense, right? She's been through enough, so I lie. "I'm just really happy to see you." She nods and smiles.

We get to work. Audrey sent over some spreadsheets. We discussed the site plans, and Olivia checked the vendor's requirements. They give me headaches.

By NOON, I check my watch. "I need to head back. Grabbing lunch with the girls and Hannah. I'm taking her to the airport after." Olivia nods without looking up. "Of course. Go."

When I get home, I hear Hannah before I see her. "No, that's unacceptable. You've had me on hold for thirty minutes, and now you're telling me there's no other flight out today?" She's pacing the hall barefoot in yoga pants and a tank, damp hair twisted up, skin still flushed from the shower. "What's going on?" I ask.

"Flight's canceled. Storm system over the city. Nothing out till tomorrow." She's clearly pissed. "I've been trying everything. I might have to stay another night." I pull out my phone.

"Let me check." She's right. Since nothing is going out today, I booked her the earliest flight for tomorrow and texted Olivia.

> Me: Change of plans. Hannah's flight got canceled. She's staying one more night. Booked her for one tomorrow. Sorry.

> Olivia: Totally understand. Thanks for the update.

That's it. No emoji. No extra word. But I can read it.

REMINDER: BEER TASTING WITH JOSH &
AUDREY – 6 PM.

Shit. Shit. Shit.

> Olivia: Forgot we're tasting beers
> tonight with J&A. Totally fine if you
> can't make it.

> Me: Shit. Forgot too. Let me check
> with Hannah, and I'll let you know.

I knock on the guest house bathroom door. Push it
open without thinking. "Hey, Han—" She's standing in
front of the mirror in just panties, brushing her hair out.
She turns slightly, catches my stare. "What's up?"

I freeze. "Sorry. I didn't—"

"Ethan," she says, raising an eyebrow. "You've seen
me naked a thousand times. You're fine." I look away.
"Yeah. I just... don't know what the rules are anymore."
She walks past me toward the closet, still topless. "We're
on a break, not divorced. You're still my husband. Don't
act like you haven't looked already." She smirks.

And yeah. I've looked because she's beautiful. And
because my body still remembers what it was like to be
hers. But that's not the point. "I have a work thing
tonight. Beer tasting for the bar," I say. She glances over
her shoulder. "Sounds fun. I'll come."

"I was actually hoping you could stay with the girls."
She stops. "Seriously? You want me to stay back, alone,
with the kids, on my last night here?"

"It's just work." She tilts her head. "Is that code for
Olivia is going to be there?"

"It's a work thing, so yes, she's going to be there." She takes a step closer, presses a kiss to my mouth, smiling. That smile felt like a warning. "Let me get dressed. I'll be ready in ten."

This night is going to be a nightmare. I walk outside and call Liv. She answers way too coldly, "Hey."

"I need to tell you something, please don't be mad. Hannah wants to come to the tasting tonight." Pause. "You invited her?"

"No. She just... said if it's work, she should be welcome."

"She's not wrong," Olivia says, clipped. "You okay?" I don't even know why I asked that. Of course, she's not okay. I'm not OK either. "No, Ethan. But I'll manage."

"Liv, I didn't plan this."

"I know. But you didn't stop it, either. I've got to go. See you later."

She hangs up, and I just know I fucked up. Everything is fucked up. Hannah's already dressed when I go back inside. "Ready?" She's ready to be a total bitch in the nicest way possible. I nod and get going.

AT THE BAR, the vibe dies the second we walk in. Josh, Audrey, Lily, Julia, and Olivia are all mid-laugh. "Hey, everyone," I start, voice rough. "This is—"

"Hannah," she cuts in brightly, waving like a game

show host. "The wife, baby mama, and the outsider judge of beers today." She laughs like it's the funniest joke on earth, and everyone seems to enjoy it, except for Julia and Olivia. She just looked at me like she might kill me later, and I deserve it.

This is a mess, but it's *my* mess.

Hannah makes a beeline for her. "You must be Olivia." Oh fuck, I'm so fucking scared right now. But I only hear, "Likewise." They're being polite and controlled. Hannah spins back toward me. "This is already fun." No, it's not.

We sit, start drinking, and taste different ABVs and bitterness levels while the brewer explains every detail of each beer. Josh talks about hops. Audrey steers the ship. But I can feel the whole table vibrating. Hannah and Olivia disagree on a stout. Hannah says it's complex. Olivia calls it bitter. The subtext is loud. They're not talking about beers anymore. They are giving each other adjectives. Fuck me.

By the end, we've tried ten beers, and everyone's faking normal. Audrey calls it. "That's a wrap. I'll send the finalized list tomorrow."

Olivia stands. "That's good night for me. Julia, you are coming?" Julia hesitates, "I think I'll stay." Lily smiles. Audrey's already grabbing her bag. "I'm out."

Olivia gives everyone a nod, then finally turns to me, gives me a kiss on the cheek, and whispers, "Goodnight, Ethan." Hannah saw her, and I know she intended to do it when she was just far enough that she couldn't say or do anything. But now, she looks pissed.

They're both doing things to just fuck me over. I deserve it.

We start walking towards the truck. "I can see the appeal, and the resemblance, too. You definitely have a type." I ignore it. "Also, quick question, Ethan." I stare at her, but I know what's coming. "Are you sleeping with her?" Oh, here we fucking go.

"Hannah, don't." I'm way too buzzed to do this right now, and I sure as hell don't want to have a fight with my wife about my girlfriend. "Don't what? Ask the question I already know the answer to?" We discussed this, and she said no questions. I should've known better.

"We agreed. No questions." She stares me down. "Got it. That's all I needed to hear." We drive in silence.

When we get to the house, everything is quiet. Hannah and I walk into the guesthouse, and she turns to me. "Can we talk?"

"There's nothing to talk about," I mutter, already tired. "You said no questions. We agreed to that, so why are you asking things now?"

"I know what we agreed on, Ethan. It was my goddamn idea." Her voice cracks, but she holds her ground. "I didn't want to be here like this. But I am. And I see what's going on."

I drag a hand through my hair. "What do you want?"

"I want the truth. Well, honestly, I want a lot of things." She says, and I look at her for a long beat.

"What exactly do you want, Hannah?" Her eyes don't waver. She stands her ground. "I want my husband to fuck me." I blink. "What?"

"I want you. I want to feel something again. I want to stop wondering if I ever mattered. I want to know if there's anything left here, between us." My chest tightens. "I also wanna know if there's something here, but we can't do this."

"Why? Because you're fucking her?" I flinch, and she sees it. Fuck. I didn't want her to find out about it this way. "Can we talk about this later? When we're both sober."

Her face shifts. "No, we're talking about it right now. You used to look at me like I was it for you. Like I was home. I haven't felt that in a long time." I don't know what I'm doing. I don't want her to feel like this. She is still my wife, the mother of my kids. And I don't even know what's going to happen after this month ends.

What if Olivia says she wants nothing more to do with me? What if Hannah still wants me? Fuck, what if I still wish to be with Hannah after all of this? I stop thinking. I reach for her and kiss her. Not because I'm confused, but because I fucking love this woman.

My hands find her waist, and her mouth finds mine. The kiss is rough, tangled in guilt. She pulls at my shirt like she's angry with it, and I let her. My hands slide up her back. Her skin is familiar and foreign all at once. My heart's screaming at me to stop, but my body's already moving. She pulls her top over her head. I follow suit. It's like watching a car crash is about to happen, and still pressing the gas.

She yanks me closer, breath hot against my neck. Her hands shake when she undoes my jeans.

Her back hits the table, and the rest of the clothes hit the floor. My sanity fucking goes out of my body. She's not used to having sex like this. She doesn't even like it like this. But she hasn't stopped me. Which means she wants to prove something, and I might let her.

I start touching her, but I stop. "Hannah, I love you, but I don't know if we should..." She kisses me harder, pulls me closer, and whispers, "Just fuck me, Ethan, don't think, don't talk." The table is about to collapse, so I grab her and throw her onto the couch. She smiles at me, and that undoes me. I get on top of her and start touching her. Grabbing her breasts, biting her nipples, she's losing it.

"Please, I want you inside," she says, pulling me closer, and I do. I slide into her, and it's everything I remember. The heat, the tightness, that overwhelming wave that used to mean love. Now it just feels like drowning, but I love it. She gasps my name, and it clutches me like I'm something worth keeping. I hold her hips like I'm trying to convince myself of the same.

She feels so good that for a moment, I forget everything and give it all to her. Because she deserves this, she deserves it all.

I stay there for a second, after we're finished, my forehead pressed to hers, both of us still catching our breath. My stomach's already turning. This wasn't supposed to happen. I don't know what the hell I was thinking. Well, I wasn't. That's the problem.

Her fingers comb through my hair gently, like nothing's broken. And I can't even look her in the eye.

CHAPTER THIRTY-THREE
OLIVIA

I wake up angry.

Not throw-a-vase mad. Not even cry-into-your-pillow mad. Just that simmering, bone-deep, low-level rage that creeps in before your feet even hit the floor.

My mind goes to Hannah laughing at the bar like she owned the place. Like she hadn't hijacked the night with her casual 'wife and baby mama' declaration like it was a damn party trick. And Ethan? Just standing there. Jaw tight, lips sealed, saying absolutely nothing.

I grab my phone. No message from him. Of course not. Must be too busy choking on guilt or still playing house with his actual wife.

"Whatever," I mutter to the void, but it sounds so hollow. Because I know it's not *whatever*. It's never been *whatever*. Julia knocks once, purely for formality, and waltzes in.

She's holding two mugs, both steaming. "Coffee," she declares, handing one over like a peace offering. "And before you ask, yes, I spiked it. I figured you'd need something stronger than caffeine." I take it, grateful. "Thanks. You were not wrong." She flops onto the bed beside me, messy bun listing slightly to the side, hoodie sleeves pushed up.

"You want to talk about last night?" she asks, voice cautious but teasing. "Because I'm still processing the part where she introduced herself like a Real Housewives tagline." I snort, despite myself. "The wife, the baby mama."

Julia raises an eyebrow. "Wow. That was alarmingly accurate. Should I be concerned you've been rehearsing?" I shrug, take a sip of the spiked coffee, and it burns a little, exactly the way I need it to. "You cope your way, I cope mine."

She laughs, and it feels good, that short, honest kind of laugh that shakes something loose inside me. At this point, what else can I do?

I know who she is and what she is. She knows what and who I am. We all played our parts last night. She is the wife, and I'm the ghost —the mistake. It's messy, unfair, and widely uncomfortable. And maybe, deep down, some part of me knew it was always going to end like this.

I glance at Julia, who's now scrolling through her phone, humming like this is just another morning. "It's fine," I say quietly, mostly to myself. "I'll be fine."

She looks up, eyes soft but skeptical. "You always are," she says.

And I want to believe her. I really do.

LATER, I'm halfway through an email when my phone buzzes. His name lights up the screen.

> Ethan: Hey. How are you? Can we meet for lunch?

Oh, now he wants to talk. For a full minute, I just stare at the message, fingers hovering over the keyboard. I can practically feel my pulse in my thumb. Then I type back before I can talk myself out of it.

> Me: Busy, but yeah, we can meet.

The second I hit send, I regret it. But I go anyway. Because apparently, I'm still that kind of idiot. The café is small, tucked near the site, all warm light and burnt espresso. He's already there when I walk in, sitting by the window, same black T-shirt, same tired hands wrapped around a mug he's probably not even drinking.

He looks like hell. Unshaven, eyes bruised from lack of sleep. I don't ask. I'm not sure I want to hear the answer. I slide into the seat across from him, set my phone on the table, and stir my iced coffee to have something to do. He leans forward, voice low. "Liv, I'm sorry."

I shake my head immediately. "You don't need to apologize."

"I do. I shouldn't have let her go to the tasting. The comments, the looks, all of it was out of line." The way he says it, so softly, almost undoes me, but I keep my face neutral. I sip my drink, the ice clinking against the glass. "Let's just keep this simple. While we still can. I can't even imagine how she must have felt, seeing me there. Having to talk to me. I know how I felt. And it wasn't great. So let's leave it at that."

He nods slowly but doesn't look away. His eyes are fixed on me like he's trying to read between the words, to find the version of me that used to reach back. I don't give him anything. Not a smile, not a lifeline.

When we finally finish, I slide out of the booth, drop a few bills on the table, and sling my bag over my shoulder. "I'm heading to the site," I say, keeping my tone easy, businesslike. "Need to catch Audrey before she leaves." He pushes back his chair. "I'll come with." Oh, great. Because what I really need right now is time alone in a truck with him after last night.

It's weirdly quiet when we get there. Same as the ride here. The kind that makes you hyper-aware of how close you're standing to someone you shouldn't be at all.

The site looks almost peaceful, the skeleton of the bar catching the afternoon light, the faint sound of construction somewhere down the block. A breeze moves through, kicking up dust and paper. We walk toward the back, both pretending we're fine. He's talking about timelines, supply delays, and something about paint colors. I nod at the right moments, half-listening, half-counting my breaths.

Then his hand finds my waist, casual, familiar, too easy, and for a split second, my body remembers before my mind can shut it down. And thank God, that's when Audrey shows up. "Hey, sorry I'm late," she calls out, and I could honestly kiss her.

We both step back like guilty teenagers. Ethan clears his throat. I open my notebook like it's a shield. We spread out on one of the picnic tables, printouts, floor plans, and lists of last-minute orders. Audrey starts talking through deliveries, permits, and staffing. I nod, take notes, throw myself into the details because that's the only safe thing left to hold onto. We keep it professional.

We talk about lighting fixtures, signage, and marketing rollouts. Every word measured, every glance edited down to something neutral. When we finish, Audrey packs up her things, waves, and heads off. The silence that follows is sharp enough to cut through the noise of traffic in the distance.

I can feel him watching me, waiting for something I'm not going to give. So I gather the papers, tuck them under my arm, and keep walking.

THAT NIGHT, he texted. Again.

> Ethan: Dinner with the girls at my dad's. You still in?

I forgot I agreed to this. By now, everybody knows we are kind of together, because they are on a 'break', but it still feels wrong, and weird. I stare at the screen for a second, then type back.

> Me: Yeah. Be there.

I shower, throw on a cute but not trying-too-hard outfit, and toss a couple of craft kits into a gift bag. When I get there, the girls run straight into my arms like I've known them forever. We watch Barbie Mermaid something, eat spaghetti, and I help them color paper crowns while Hannah's name lingers like a shadow I'm trying not to look at too closely.

Later, on the porch, Ethan walks me to my car. His kiss is soft. "Wanna stay the night?" I almost let myself stay. But I don't. "Night, Ethan." He nods.

I drive home alone. Windows down.

The heart is doing that stupid thing where it hurts and hopes at the same time.

IT's BEEN over three weeks since the girls came here, and they have been fantastic.

We agreed to have lunch with Agnes a while back, and today is finally the day. When she shows up, I get it. She's smart, funny, and dry as hell. Protective of Ethan like a sister who's been through the war with him, and maybe she has. I like her. Which honestly pisses me off a little. I wasn't looking to like her since she's so close with Hannah.

She watches Ethan laugh at something dumb I say, then turns to me like she's sizing me up. "He's never looked at anyone the way he looks at you," she says. "Not even close." And I believe her because I know that look.

"I know this isn't my place, and I should just shut my mouth, but he loves you." I don't say anything. That's not news for me.

"He is conflicted, between you two. He's taking this time to really figure his feelings out, but I know he loves both of you." That makes my heart skip a beat. I know he still loves her, I know that his perfect world is to have both of us, and not in a sexy male fantasy. In a 'let's figure this out' kind of way. And honestly, I admire him for it. Not everyone can admit they love two women at the same time, let alone their first love and their wife. But, is it fair? Absolutely not.

THAT NIGHT, she stays with the girls. Ethan and I end up at my place.

When the door closed, we're on each other. His hands on my waist, mine already in his hair. We don't speak, because what's left to say? We both know these days have been hard. We haven't had time for ourselves, but we don't need to linger there. We don't have to over-explain what we both know.

My dress is gone. His shirt's gone. He lifts me like it's nothing, like I'm not breaking open a little more every time he touches me like this. His mouth is on mine before I can think, and that's the point. I don't want to think.

Then he slides in. One deep, slow thrust that knocks the air out of me. "Fuck," I breathe. He groans against my neck, and then we're moving. He says my name like a vow, and I kiss him to shut him up. His hips slam into mine like he's angry about it. I bite down on his shoulder because if I don't, I'll scream.

His hand slips between us. "Come for me," he whispers. And I do. It hits hard and fast, like a fuse snapping. I arch. He holds me up through it. Keeps going until I feel him pulse inside me, his breath sharp and ragged in my ear.

We don't talk after we're done. This didn't feel like it always does. Something has changed, and I already know tomorrow's going to hurt.

But we kept having sex. Maybe because we enjoy it, perhaps because we missed each other, or maybe because neither of us wants to talk.

And if we stop, we'll talk.

THE MORNING COMES QUICKLY, and neither of us wants to cook, so we decide to head to Lily's for coffee and breakfast.

This place has changed a lot since we used to come here. It has been passed down for generations, and now my hopefully future sister-in-law runs it.

His phone buzzes when we are mid-conversation, and I know it's her for the look he gives me. "Hannah asked me to call her. I'll be right back," I nod, trying not to let it show. But I'm pissed, it's like every time we are having fun, or having a moment, or just enjoying our company, she's there.

I watch as he steps outside to make the call. I can see him walking back and forth, hand through his hair. He looks pissed. Confused? I don't know what's happening, but whatever it is can't be good.

He comes back, and he's pale as a ghost. His jaw is tight, and he's not even speaking. "Ethan?" I sit up straighter. "What is it? What's wrong?" He won't look at me. What the fuck is happening? My stomach drops, I feel nauseous. I've never seen him like this.

"Ethan, you're scaring me. What's happening? Did something happen to the girls? Is Hannah okay?" He looks at me, and I can see the pain behind his eyes.

"Hannah's pregnant."

"Pregnant?" I repeat—maybe the word will change if I say it more slowly. "Who's the—" I stop myself. I don't need the rest of that sentence. I see it all over his face.

I'm going to be sick.

"*You*," I whisper. "You're the father." He doesn't say a damn word, and that's the confirmation I needed. There's just silence. I stand too fast, so fast the whole place spins around me. I feel dizzy, but I brace myself against the table.

"When?" I ask. It comes out too soft. I ask again, louder this time. "When did this happen?" He scrubs a hand over his face. He doesn't look at me. He can't even face me right now. "The last night she was here. We—"

"Stop," I can't hear this from him. He was with me before she got here. He was in *my* bed. He told me he couldn't stay away from *me*, that he wanted *me*. He made me feel like I was the goddamn center of the universe. And meanwhile, just after a few beers, he goes straight to her.

God, I feel like such an idiot. How could I fall for it? For him again? I knew better. I always did.

"Liv—"

"No." My voice breaks. "You don't get to say my name anymore."

He finally looks at me, and it just hurts. His eyes are glassy. His face is wrecked. He looks like the one who got broken. Too bad I already beat him to it. "I was never going to ask you to choose," I say, quiet now. "Not between me and her. Not your kids. I knew what I was signing up for." I swallow hard. "But I never thought you'd do this to me. We were supposed to figure things out, *together*."

"It wasn't— I didn't plan it. It just... happened," he says, like that changes anything.

"Oh, great. That helps. You just happened to get your wife pregnant while having an affair with your ex-girlfriend."

"Don't call it that, Liv. And I know it makes it worse." I nod, because he's right. It does. Tears sting my eyes, but I refuse to cry in front of him. "You had a choice," I say. "That night, you chose to do it, you chose her." He opens his mouth, maybe to explain, maybe to beg, but I'm already done.

"My fucking heart was in your hands, Ethan, and you dropped it. Again." He moves closer to me. "Liv, please—"

"You know what? Don't." I cut in, sharp. "Your free trial's over."

I don't look back as I walk out of the restaurant. I can't.

Because if I do, I'll fall apart right there, and he doesn't get that version of me, not *anymore*.

My legs move, but my mind's spinning. Hannah's pregnant, with his baby. She is his wife, and they are growing their family.

God, I'm such a fucking idiot.

I can still feel him on my skin from last night, I can still taste him on my lips.

But he's not mine anymore.

He never was.

CHAPTER THIRTY-FOUR
ETHAN

THE SECOND OLIVIA WALKS AWAY, IT HITS ME.

It felt like a hollow, wide-open kind of pain. Like someone reached in, grabbed my heart from me, and yanked it out of my chest.

She didn't yell at me, she didn't cry, and that's how I know she hates me.

She looked like she didn't recognize me anymore. I'm still sitting there in the restaurant, while the world just slipped through my hands. I can't fucking breathe.

Hannah's pregnant, and Olivia is gone.

I stare at my phone, hands shaking, vision blurry. I scroll aimlessly, not even sure what I'm looking for. I need a voice that won't make it worse.

AGNES

I hit call before I can overthink it— it rings for a second time, and she picks up. "Hey, I know, I know, you miss me," she says jokingly. "She's pregnant, Agnes. Hannah. And it's mine. I just told Olivia and..." I exhale hard. "I think I lost her. I think I really fucking lost her."

She's quiet for a bit. "Where are you? Are you driving? If so, pull over. Breathe." I breathe in and out as I head to my car. "No, I'm— I was having breakfast with Olivia. I'm in the car, but I'm not driving."

"Okay, breathe. Tell me what happened." I tell her about the night at the beer tasting, the tension between them, how things escalated when we got home. How I fucked everything up. "She wanted another baby," I say, like it's some twisted punchline. "I told her no, and I meant it. We talked about this but, I didn't want to bring another child into the world when all this confusion was consuming me." I exhale.

"One fucking night." She's just listening on the other line. Not judging me or anything. "What happened with Olivia?"

"I saw the pain in her face. I hurt her worse than I did in the past. She's gone, Agnes. And I can't even blame her. This was all my fault." There's silence, that I know it's pity. "She loves you, Ethan."

"Not anymore, Agnes. She's long gone." I drag a hand down my face. "What kind of man does this?" I whisper. "Cheats on his wife, falls back in love with the girl he never truly stopped loving, and then knocks up his wife on the way out?"

"You weren't exactly cheating," she says. "You and Hannah were on a break." I laugh, but there's no humor in it. "Does that even matter?" She stays silent, and we both know the answer. Of course, it doesn't matter. Hannah knows I was with Olivia. But that doesn't change the truth. I messed this up for both of them.

"Do you still love Hannah?" she asks. I hesitate. Too long. "I love that she's the mother of my girls. I love what we used to have. And yes, I do love her, but I'm not in love with her. Not anymore. Haven't been in a long time, I think. Way before seeing Liv again." She sighs. I know she wants to yell at me, and she's not doing it just because I'm losing it. "The worst part is that I'm not even happy about this baby. Isn't that fucked? I love my girls, I live and breathe for them, but I don't feel that way about this child. What kind of man am I?"

"All I know is that you're not a bad one, Ethan," she says. "You are conflicted, frustrated, sad, but this doesn't mean you're not going to love that child. You are a great father." I close my eyes and try not to cry.

We ended the call, and I started driving. I don't even remember half of it. My hands are shaking; my heart is pounding in my chest as I walk towards her door. I don't know what the fuck I'm doing here. But I need to talk to her. I knock once. No response. I knock again. She opens the door, looking me dead in the eyes, arms crossed.

"Liv," I whisper.

She takes a step back, silent. She lets me in, but I can see it on her face. I'm the last person she wants to see. I stay standing there, even though my legs feel like they're going to give up on me. "I'm sorry," I say. "I know it's not enough, and nothing right now will be, but I am sorry."

"I talked to Hannah. It's over between us. I should've ended it a long time ago, but I didn't. I was trying to be decent. Trying to do the right thing. But I screwed everything up instead." She stares at me. "So now you end your marriage?" she finally says. "Now that she's pregnant? Wow, how classy, Ethan."

"No, I'm ending it because it should've ended a long time ago. Not just because of you. Because I've been lying to her, to myself, but this doesn't change how I feel about you." Her jaw tightens. She turns away, as if looking at me is too much. "I love you," I say. "I've loved you since we were kids. That hasn't changed."

She turns back, eyes glassy. But there's no softness in them. Just pain. "You think saying that fixes all of this?"

"No, I know this doesn't fix shit," I say. "But we need to be honest and say our truths."

"Oh, you want the truth?" Her voice cracks open. "Here's the truth. I loved you, Ethan, for years. I thought about you, *fuck*, I even dreamt about you. I stalked you on social media, and I saw that you were happy. I followed along with your wedding, the baby showers, and the birth of your girls, and I was proud of *you*. Jealous of *her*, but happy for *you*. I saw the man you turned out to be. And while I wanted that with you, I settled for my life."

She sighs and takes another step back. "When your mother died, I suffered, and I hesitated on coming here because I didn't want to see you. Because I knew this could happen. I knew I'd fall for you all over again. And I did. I even became the other woman, for fucks sake, we had an affair for weeks. And even after my divorce, I was still 'the other one'. I gave you everything, and you still broke me." She looks exhausted.

"I didn't mean to—"

"You didn't mean to get her pregnant either, right?"

"No," I say. "I didn't."

"But it still happened." I nod. Because what else can I do? "I won't be the reason your marriage ends. I won't be the villain in your daughter's story. I won't do that. Not to them, not to her, and not to myself."

"You're not the villain," I say, stepping forward. "You didn't ruin anything. It was already broken." She laughs, bitter.

"I'm not asking you to forgive me. I just needed you to know I'm not walking away from you. I never wanted to." She stares at me like she's trying to remember who I used to be.

"Then why did you?" she says. "I didn't mean to."

"Don't—" she says, holding up a hand. "You said we'd take it moment by moment, that we'd figure it out. And I believed you. I was building something again... for me, for my kids, for us. And now..." Her voice breaks. "Now I feel like a goddamn idiot."

"You're not," I say, voice hoarse. "You're everything." She closes her eyes. Breath shaky. "Then why does it feel like I'm the one who lost everything— *again*?" She walks towards the end table and grabs an envelope and the box my mom left her.

We haven't talked about this in a while, and we never discussed what was in that box. She grabs it and hands it to me.

The room goes quiet. All I can hear is my heart pounding. When I opened the box, my world shattered. It was my mom's engagement ring. She wanted Olivia to have it, no matter whether I ever gave it to her or not. She deserves it, she always did, and now I lost the opportunity to give it to her.

"Never not yours," I whispered.

Her eyes snap open. "Ethan, don't."

"I still mean it, and this ring is supposed to be yours," I say. "You can hate me. You can shut the door. But I've never not been yours. And nothing will change that." That's when she breaks. The tears fall fast. Her whole body shakes. And I hate myself more than I ever have because I did this.

"I don't know what you want me to do with that, or with the ring. I wanted it sixteen years ago. And when she left it to me, for a second, I thought maybe it would finally be mine and mean something. But now, I can't have it," she chokes out.

I swallow hard because it's true. That ring belongs to her, but I can't force her to keep it. "You need to go."

"Please, just don't forget I love you, I always will." She wipes her face with the back of her hand. "I'll fix this," I say as a promise.

She backs away like I just set the room on fire. "Figure it out without me, Ethan. Your life is on fire, and

I'm not sticking around to watch it burn. We're done, for good this time."

And that's it. That's the line I can't come back from. I nod because she's right.

"I'm sorry," I whisper. "For everything."

"I know, I'm sorry too." I turn, and I don't look back. I cannot bear to see her like this

EPILOGUE
OLIVIA

One Year Later

THERE'S A BREEZE TODAY, soft and warm, the kind that carries the scent of sea salt and morning coffee. I stand on the terrace of our hotel and watch as the sun rises over Tacoon, casting long shadows along the stone path that winds through the garden. It's peaceful. The kind of peace I never thought I'd find here again.

The boutique hotel is finally open. After a year of paint-stained clothes, last-minute design changes, and way too many calls with vendors who couldn't meet a deadline to save their lives, it's real. And it's beautiful. I run all the marketing and social media, something I can do from anywhere, but I choose to do it here. Because here feels like mine now.

Julia's found her rhythm, too. She runs guest experience with that contagious energy only she has. She and

Lily... well, they're something. Still not labeled, not locked in, but steady in their own chaotic, fantastic way. Lily's thriving. She took over the coffee shop and made it entirely hers, with book stacks in the corners, vintage mugs, and a chalkboard wall full of hand-written poetry.

Audrey's still running the show until we find someone to take over full-time management. She says she'll hand over the reins soon, but I think part of her loves the chaos too much to let go just yet. Josh stepped back and said he needed some time to travel. He sends postcards every now and then.

The kids are happy. Like, really happy. They've settled into their routines, made friends, and joined clubs. Tacoon became their safe place, too. On weekends, we bike to the farmers' market or hike up to the overlook.

My relationship with my dad is a slow rebuild. Some days are more complicated than others, but we're showing up. That's all I can ask. Mom and I have slipped back into a more familiar routine. She makes tea some nights. I sit with her when I can, talk about nothing and everything.

And Maggie, she's family again. Somehow, through all the loss and love and pain, we've grown into this easy, quiet closeness. We don't talk about him often. We don't need to.

As for me... well, there's Matthew. A new face in town who made a move on me, and it worked.

It's quiet between us, private. We share coffee some mornings, sometimes dinner. We don't talk about labels. We don't owe anyone that. Something is comforting in the stillness of it —just two people choosing simplicity and quiet. And for now, that's what I need.

Ethan?

We've spoken just a handful of times in the past year. It's polite, careful, and kind. He left Tacoon way before the hotel launched, saying he needed to focus on his firm, the girls, Hannah, and the new baby. Another girl. I think he was happy when he said it. Tired, but happy.

He doesn't live with Hannah anymore, that much I know. They're separated, still co-parenting, still tangled in the logistics of a life too big and messy to unravel overnight. There's a lot of money involved, a lot of history. And I get it. Been there, done that.

From what I understand, Hannah's doing okay, too. Maybe that's the best any of us can hope for— okay.

He meant it, back then, when he said he didn't want that marriage. But he also meant it when he said he needed to clean up his mess first. And apparently, he is.

Sometimes I wonder if our story is truly over. If that fire we felt was meant to burn us clean, or to remind us that we're still capable of feeling that deeply. But I don't linger there long. I don't want to keep dreaming about a future we never got to have.

Life is good. It's quiet. It's mine.

And for now, that's enough.

EPILOGUE
ETHAN

THE HOUSE IS QUIETER THESE DAYS. EMPTY even.

Hannah and I are officially separated now. No lawyers breathing down our necks, no shouting matches, just two people trying to do right by the three little girls who still think the world makes sense. We kept the house for them, the backyard with the swing set, and the same bedtime routine.

I live in the studio in the back; they have the whole house. I'm slowly learning that being a good father doesn't mean pretending everything's fine; it just means showing up, even when it hurts.

The firm's doing well. Too well, maybe. I bury myself in work when the house gets too quiet, when the echoes of what I lost start getting too loud.

It's been a year since Tacoon. Since *her*.

Olivia and I have spoken a few times, polite, surface-level, careful. Texts about the project, a quick check-in around the holidays, one call on my birthday that lasted three minutes, but wrecked me for days. She sounded good. Happy, even. And that's what I wanted for her, wasn't it?

I still catch myself thinking about her sometimes when I'm driving home, when a song that she loved comes on, when I see something that would've made her laugh. The ache isn't sharp anymore. It's just... there.

I haven't dated. Not really. I've gone through the motions, a few dinners, a few polite conversations that never turn into anything. Because the truth is, no one's her.

And I don't deserve her. Maybe not yet, maybe not ever. But that doesn't change what's true. I'm still in love with her. Always have been. Probably always will be.

For now, I focus on the things I can build, my girls, my work, and myself. I try to become the kind of man she wouldn't have to heal from again. But some nights, when the house is still, and I'm the only one awake, I let myself imagine what it would feel like to see her again. To tell her that I'm finally ready, not to start over, but to keep going. Together.

Because after everything, after all the years and mistakes and distance, one thing hasn't changed.

I've loved this woman *for over twenty years.*

And I know that in twenty more, *I'll still feel exactly the same.*

NEVER NOT YOURS

BONUS CHAPTER
OLIVIA

Five Years Later

LIFE FEELS DIFFERENT THESE DAYS.

Or maybe I'm the one who's different now.

The hotel's expansion project just launched, which is a ridiculous reminder that full circles happen whether you're ready or not. A few years ago, the beginning of this project was the one thing that made me want to be in Tacoon, besides the obvious other reasons. And now, it's finally done.

Perfect time, because my agency has grown so much since moving its headquarters here. Work's non-stop now. Lily's coffee shop is now one of the biggest clients; she's even expanding outside of town.

The boys are thriving, and for the first time in a long time, life feels... steady. Peaceful, even.

Which is probably why the universe decided tonight

was the night Ethan would text me. We haven't talked in about three years, maybe even closer to four. Our last conversations were merely business. I did send a happy birthday text four years ago; he did the same. We said happy holidays, but after that... nothing.

Radio silence. Healing silence. Or so I told myself.

The thing about seeing his name on my phone is that I don't know what to expect. And I hate that my mind still goes *everywhere*.

> Ethan: Hey, how are you? I'm in town for a few days, and was wondering if you would have dinner with me? I have a place in mind, but wanted to ask you first. If you don't want to, I understand. But I would love to see you.

Oh, that's the text. See, that's the thing. This could mean so many things. It could mean, 'hey, I'm moving to Tacoon, just wanted to give you a heads up', or 'hey, we'll be working together in another project, just so you know', or whatever. Of course, my mind goes to a third option, that's more 'hey, I missed you, I still love you, and I'm sorry.' Fuck. It's been almost four years without any contact at all.

Why do I still feel like this? He hurt me so badly, and I still think about him every single day.

Anyway, I went ahead and replied like an adult who hasn't been overthinking this text and has moved on.

> Me: Hey, is there wine at this place you were thinking? Because I'll need wine.

> Ethan: There will always be wine, Liv.

'Liv', I hate that I remembered how my name sounded on his lips.

> Me: Good, send me the address and the time.

As soon as I sent that text, I regretted it. And it's not because I don't want to have dinner with him, it's just hard. We haven't seen each other in over six years, and I don't know what to expect out of this.

I've healed, I've moved on, from him, from my old life. I'm happy and content with what I have right now, thanks mainly to therapy. But we were friends once, and after all this time, I feel like we owe each other the chance to talk. And drink wine, which explains why I'm standing outside a little cliffside restaurant overlooking the water. The same water that once witnessed a very messy, foolish version of us.

I smooth my dress, inhale deeply, and step inside. He's already waiting for me.

And holy hell.

Five years have done some things to him. His beard is a little fuller, hair way shorter, shoulders broader, the kind of glow-up that makes you want to sue the universe for emotional damages.

He stands when he sees me, and something in my chest stutters violently. Nope, don't go there again.

"Liv," he says, softly. Oh shit. "Hey," I answer, even softer, because apparently my lungs have decided to stop functioning.

We sit. The waiter brings a bottle of wine. He ordered my favorite wine, but I acted like I didn't notice. We start talking about nothing and everything all at once. Like time hasn't passed, which is one of the things I hate and love most about him. We can talk for hours about everything, like we didn't hurt each other.

We talk about work and the new opportunities with the projects. About the fantastic job his stepsiblings have done. We talked about our kids, his co-parenting schedule with Hannah after the divorce, which was finalized two years ago.

I already knew this information, but I pretended to be surprised.

By the time the bottle is nearly empty, we're lighter, looser... stupid even. He leans back, smirking. "You've been avoiding me."

"Me? You haven't texted or called. I wasn't going to. But that doesn't mean I've been *avoiding* you." I say, shrugging. "It just felt safer that way."

His eyes keep dropping to my mouth when he talks, and I don't know if it's the wine or if it's seeing him again after all these years, but that's making me feel things that I don't want to feel. His smile keeps slipping into something familiar, something that lived under my skin long before I knew pain had a name. *Ethan*.

The bottle of wine turns into two, because neither of us is ready to end the conversation, or the night. "You know," he murmurs, swirling what's left on the glass, "after all this time, you're still it to me, Liv."

It hits low in my stomach, absolutely unwanted. I nod, smiling with my lips and not my heart, because we can't do this again. If I allow this conversation to continue, it will end one of two ways. On a bed, or with a heartbreak, and neither of those is a good idea right now. "Ethan, please don't. We don't have to do this again."

"Do what, Liv? Tell the truth of how we feel about each other, even after everything?" Why is he talking in the plural tense? He disappeared for years again and expects me to be okay with everything just because we shared two bottles of wine and a four-hour conversation.

"Don't put words in my mouth. Don't talk like you know what I'm thinking or feeling, because you don't."

"I'm sorry, that's not what I wanted to do. I just... I know what I feel, and what I've been thinking for the last five years, hell, for the past twenty-five years, Olivia."

This man is going to be the death of me.

"Look, I get it. You've missed me, or the idea of me, or having me. I did too, twenty-five years ago, and sixteen, and ten, and five, maybe even three years ago. But I've moved on." I can see him struggling to find the words to respond to what I just said. But he needed to hear it.

"Can I ask you a question?" Nope, you can't. "Sure," I said instead.

Fuck me.

"Do you still love me?" Well, time to be honest and hope for the best. "Of course, I still love you, Ethan. I will always love you. But that doesn't mean I want to go there again."

He nods, and I can see the pain behind his eyes. "I told you I wanted to get my shit together, and I did. I'm not expecting you to come back to me just because. But I have loved you for over twenty-five years, Olivia. We were married to other people, we had kids, and I still feel the same about you. No time can change that. I know I messed up *badly*. I know I broke your heart *twice*, and I will ask for your forgiveness forever if needed. I'm truly sorry for not loving you in the way you deserve."

And that's what hit me.

He is saying precisely what I wanted to hear years ago. I drink what's left in my wine glass, take a deep breath, and open my mouth, but nothing comes out. My mind goes blank, I can't breathe, and I can feel my eyes getting watery.

So, I swallow and nod. "Understood. Want to get going?" I nod and stand up. He sets cash on the table, and we're off.

By the time we step outside, the sun is long gone, and Tacoon feels cold and dark. We stroll toward the parking lot, neither of us moving away. If anything, we keep drifting closer, like gravity finally gave up pretending it can keep us away.

He stops first. "Liv," he whispers, like he's afraid I might run.

"It was really nice seeing you, thank you for allowing

me to talk, and say sorry again." I step closer to him. "I needed this too."

I've loved him for so long that I don't know how not to love him anymore. God, I want to kiss him so bad.

I can see everything that's left to be said in his eyes, and I swear he hears my thoughts because his hands cup my jaw, and I let out the smallest breath. But I don't move. His mouth crashes into mine, and time snaps. It's desperate and rough, years of restraint burning off in seconds. His hands are everywhere. On my waist, my hair, the small of my back, he's pulling me in like he's been waiting for this moment for all these years.

I kiss him back like I've been waiting for the same thing, because I have. I know that what we had wasn't supposed to happen, at least not in the way it did. I blamed him for a while, but I was no saint in that equation. We both made our choices. Mine weren't as bad as his.

But they were choices regardless of the result.

The world tilts when he kisses me again. My back hits his truck, and I can feel his body caging mine, heat and strength and memory all tangled up on this kiss. I tug his shirt, he groans against my mouth, and it's messy and breathless and terrifyingly perfect. "Ethan..." My voice shakes, "Are we really doing this again?"

"Liv," he murmurs, looking at me like the answer has lived in him his entire life, "I told you, I would fix my life, and be deserving of you."

My heart clenches so violently, I swear it fractures.

"And if you want me, I'm here." It's different this time. He seems so sure about what he is telling me. It feels like he has actually been working on himself for years.

He kisses me again, harder this time. His hand slides up my thigh, gripping, dragging me against him, and any part of me that thought I was 'stable' or 'mature' disintegrates on the spot.

It's like we pushed a reset button, and suddenly we're becoming something new.

He pulls back suddenly. His eyes light up, his chest rising fast, as he opens the truck bed, and I can see the setup. He has blankets, pillows, a bottle of wine, and two glasses. "Get in," he says softly. I should say no. I should walk away.

But instead, I climb up, and he follows, pulling the door shut behind us. "Didn't we do this when we were sixteen?" That's when the flashbacks come.

We were so in love back then, we still are. He had just gotten his license, and his dad bought him a truck. He picked me up with the excuse that he wanted to take me for a ride and show it to me. But secretly, he had planned a date night.

He parked in a very dark spot of town, near here, to see the stars.

They looked exactly the way they look today.

"We did," he said, smiling now.

He had a setup just like this one, except we had beer that night. We weren't allowed to drink yet, so he stole it from his dad. We kept talking all night, and we ended up having sex on the truck bed. That was our first time. After that, we became inseparable. "So, you planned this?"

"I was feeling hopeful." His hands frame my face as he kisses me again, slower now.

His other hand slides up my thigh, gliding under the hem of my dress, fingers tracing inside until I shiver against his mouth. I tug him closer, pulling him between my legs, dress riding up over my thighs, and he groans. A deep, broken sound that goes straight through me. "Liv..." His voice is low, desperate. "I've missed you. You have no idea."

"I do," I whisper, nipping at his lower lip. "I really do."

His hands slide down my sides, fingers digging into my hips as he pulls me closer until my back hits the pillow. My legs part for him without question, instinct, or muscle memory; I don't even know at this point. I gasp into his mouth, but he doesn't break the kiss.

The word breaks. His forehead drops to my neck, his breath is hot, and his lips brush the place just under my ear. "I've been dreaming about this," he admits, voice low and wrecked. "About you, about the sounds you make, about how you say my name when you c—" I cut him off with a kiss, because if he says one more thing like that, I'm going to climb onto his lap and ruin every good decision I've made in five years.

He pulls back just enough to look at me, thumb brushing my lower lip. "You're shaking." I nod, "It's just the cold." His hand slides higher, fingers grabbing my panties. He is looking at me like he's asking for permission, and my hips jump toward him before I can stop myself.

He kisses me again, hotter this time, teeth grazing my lower lip, tongue sliding against mine in a way that makes my entire body arch into him. His hand tightens again, dragging me forward, pulling me into his lap with a force that knocks a breathless sound out of me. I straddle him, dress riding up, heart racing like it's about to combust. He drags his mouth down my neck, biting gently, my fingers slide under his shirt, palms skimming hot skin, and he shivers —actually shivers.

His voice cracks. "God, you're going to kill me."

"Then die for me," I whisper, and kiss him again, and then his fingers dig into my hips hard enough to leave marks as he slides into me.

I gasp, but I can't feel the air coming back into my body. I tug his hair, hard, and he groans into my throat like I'm the only thing keeping him alive. And then he slides into me.

The truck shifts slightly. People might see us, but I don't care. He doesn't either. "Liv..." he actually chokes on it.

There was a sound— somewhere between a groan and a curse, as his grip on me turned possessive, desperate. He pulls me against him so sharply I gasp. His forehead presses to mine, breaths crashing together, bodies locked tight. I breathe, rolling my hips again. Faster this time.

"I've wanted you like this," he whispers, voice

breaking with it. "A thousand damn nights. And now you're... fuck—" I kiss him to shut him up, to taste the years we pretended this wouldn't happen again.

His hands slam to my hips, dragging me harder against him, our breaths breaking, bodies moving in a rhythm that shouldn't feel this familiar after so long. The truck rocks again, it's not subtle anymore, and it's more than enough to make heat race through me.

His voice drops to a whisper, the kind that lands right in the center of my chest and doesn't ask permission to stay. "I could have burned my whole life down, started over, and I'd still never stop loving you."

The words hit me. This time, they don't feel reckless. They don't feel borrowed or temporary. They feel earned, scraped together from all the versions of him I loved, lost, mourned, and somehow still carried with me like a bruise that never faded.

"Ethan, I'm going to—" and before I can finish that sentence, I can feel him grabbing me in the way that tells me he is about to finish, and I melt in his arms.

He pulls me into a kiss, not the hungry, frantic kind we've drowned in before, but something sweeter. Something that feels like a promise. It's slow, devastating, and full of every moment we didn't get right the last time. Every almost. Every 'I'm sorry'. Every 'I miss you' that neither of us sent but both of us felt anyway.

We broke apart, cleaned ourselves up, and just stared at each other.

The noise, the years, the hurt... all of it dissolves into a single, breathless moment where it's just him and me.

"This feels exactly like that night." I can't stop thinking about all the good we had together. And for the first time, it's like I can allow myself to let the bad in the past.

We are just two people figuring life out after messy relationships, but we were something back then. We saw an opportunity to be more, and we took it. "What's on your mind, Liv?" I don't even think about it, I start talking.

"That we tried this the wrong way six years ago. We weren't in the right space, and it wasn't our time." He looks at me, confused but in a good way, if that makes sense. "Are you saying that this might be our time now?" Maybe we aren't falling back into old patterns.

"I'm saying that we have what it takes to make it work, but we need to be in it." Maybe we're stepping into something new. Something we earned. Something real. "Liv, I'm in it. You are my everything, and I'm not losing you again, *ever*." Something feels like us after all this time, and I'm choosing to pursue it.

I kiss him, but he breaks the kiss.

"Wait," he says, looking for something, but it's so dark I can barely see what the hell he's doing until I see a box.

"Olivia, love of my life, will you be mine *again*, forever this time?"

I can't help it, I start crying and laughing at the same time. He's not asking me to be his something. He is asking me to be his *everything*.

When he opens it, I see it.

Larna's ring.

And for the first time in twenty-five years, hope doesn't feel like a mistake.

ACKNOWLEDGMENTS

To everyone who ever believed in me, even when I didn't. To those who were patient, even when "one more hour" of writing turned into multiple hours and even more coffees or glasses of wine.

This book exists because of your love and faith in me.

ABOUT THE AUTHOR

I'm K.V. Thorn, a thirty-something just out here living and enjoying life. I've been writing since I was ten years old, though back then it was mostly school assignments and secret stories I never let anyone read.

With my debut romance novel, I wanted to capture love in all its forms: joy, heartbreak, grief, betrayal, and everything in between.

I'm the kind of writer who always has a few projects going at once *(my brain doesn't know how to focus on one thing)*, but this story has been with me for a long time.

I'm proud of it, I'm excited about it, and if I'm honest, I'm a little terrified to finally share it with the world.

With love, K.V. Thorn

ALSO BY K.V. THORN

Coming Next:

Love In Transit Series

NEVER NOT YOURS

K.V. THORN

THORN PUBLISHING HOUSE